The

By:

Michelle Dare

The Azure Kingdom
Michelle Dare
Published by Michelle Dare
Copyright ©2016 Michelle Dare

First Edition - published 2016
Cover Design by J.M Rising Horse Creations
Stock Photo by Dollar Photo Club
Interior Design & Proofreading by Riane Holt
Editing by Barren Acres Editing

Michelle Dare
Email: authormichelledare@gmail.com
Twitter: @michelle_dare
Facebook: https://www.facebook.com/authormichelledare
Website: http://michelledare.com/

One key, one door, one man, one leap.

Alison Wescot inherited the antique store the day her mother died. It was nothing she wanted, but she couldn't part with it. The antiques inside were all she had left of her mother. She thought she knew every piece in the store, until one day she discovered a box with a key inside, along with a letter from her mother. A key to a door she never knew existed.

Lucas Azure is the leader of the kingdom's elite guard, a group of men whose sole purpose was to protect their territory and people. The youngest of the king's four children, he was also the deadliest. The men in his group followed him faithfully, never questioning his orders. When Alison appeared, he knew he had to protect her at all costs.

The day Alison walked through the door, her recurring dream became a reality. The man who always remained a mystery was standing before her. There were dragons flying overhead and a castle in the distance. She was now in the Azure Kingdom.

Acknowledgements

My husband, my children, and my family make writing possible. My husband knows how much I love to write and picks up the slack when I'm doing so. My kids have a little less time with me, and I can only hope one day they are proud of what I've accomplished. I love them all!

Shannon, another book, another declaration of love for you. Thank you for always being there.

Stephanie and Laura, you two help me in so many ways. I appreciate you more than you know.

My betas are awesome and gave me great feedback to help make this book what it is. Crissy, Sharon, Lianne, Natalie, Lisa, Laura, Jeneane, Rebecca, Mary, Stephanie, and Jennifer, thank you for beta reading this book for me.

To my street team, thank you for everything you do. I'm so fortunate to have you on my team.

Zolie, Mecca, and Michele, you are wonderful friends. Thank you for always listening and supporting me.

To Karen, Jennifer, and Riane, this book looks as great as it does because of you. Thank you so much for your hard work.

The book community is made up of wonderful authors, bloggers, and readers. Thank you to each person who has shared, read, reviewed, and supported me.

I have so much love for all you!

This book is very different from the others I've written. I didn't know how I'd like writing fantasy, but I absolutely loved it and hope to write more in this genre. Thank you for reading and I hope you loved Ali and Luke as much as I do!

CHAPTER ONE

Discovery

My eyes fly open and I immediately sit up. I'm scanning the room, trying to find him, the man on top of the hill. Then I realize I'm not in the field of azure flowers. Reality comes crashing down around me. I'm in my bedroom. My skin is covered in a sheen of sweat, and my heart is beating so fast, it's like it's going to pound right out of my chest. The recurrent dream is so real that every time I wake, I have to remember I'm not living it; it was only in my mind.

Lying back down, my eyes close, and I try to calm my racing heart. Maybe by some crazy chance I can fall back into the dream. Unfortunately, I'm not that lucky. After tossing and turning for who knows how long, I realize I can't, however, I replay it all behind closed eyes.

I emerge from a small house and turn to look it over. It's an old cottage with a weathered, slate blue wooden door and colorful ivy covering the exterior walls. The air is warm, but not humid, and the sun is shining down, heating my skin to chase away the chill I have at being in a strange place. The second my feet hit the grass, the cottage disappears, and I'm left in a field of the most beautiful blue flowers. They are nothing like I've ever seen. The flowers remind me of miniature sunflowers with a color that resembles a clear sky on a summer day. Oddly, they aren't fragrant.

My fingers gently graze their silky petals. I'm so amazed by the flowers that I don't see the man standing in the distance. It's only when I hear a sound, like I've never heard before, that I notice him. A loud roar pierces the air, which makes the tiny hairs on the back of my neck stand up.

My gaze is fully on them now. The man's face is shadowed by a dragon, but his armor is clear, as well as his outline. I can't make out the intricacies of it from my place down the hill, but notice the steel blue color of it, and how it appears to fit close to his body. He's also wearing a cape which is billowing behind him in the breeze. Heat spreads through my body at the sight of him. There's something about him that sets my body ablaze, even from this far away. A connection to him I can't explain.

By his side is a creature I've only seen in movies or imagined from reading, a mostly white dragon.

Variances of grey scales blend in with the white ones to make it something I can only describe as majestic. Against the azure flowers the dragon stunningly stands out. Its wings are moving in a fluid motion behind the man as it roars again. Horns stick out all around its head, giving off the aura of deadliness. Strangely, I'm not afraid. I'm eerily calm. That is, until the man extends his arm and uses his hand to beckon me forward. I hear his voice like a whisper on the wind. It's captivating, making me want to go toward him, but why does he want me near?

My fear starts to kick in as I take hesitant steps, unsure if I'm making the right decision to go forward. Even as my mind argues that this might not be the wisest decision, my feet keep moving. I'm no longer in control of my body. When it doesn't seem like I'm walking fast enough, I break into a sprint. There is something inside my heart that whispers how important it is that I get to him. My mind and heart are at war with one another, but my heart ultimately wins. I need to stand beside him. He will protect me. From what, I'm not sure.

I'm running, only I'm not getting any closer. No matter how fast I move, I can't reach him. I extend my hand toward him as he does the same. It seems as if we're miles apart. He is forever untouchable.

That's when I wake up, as I just did, due to the exertion in my dream. I'm panting like I was really running. Each time I have the dream, it's like the first time I'm having it, discovering everything anew. It's always the same dream, too. This dream is different from all of my others, though. I've had recurring dreams before, but they've never felt so real. I want to get back into this dream and find him. It feels imperative to my survival that I do so.

Opening my eyes again, I glance at the alarm clock beside my bed. Seven in the morning. I don't have to open the store for two more hours. What I should do is go back to sleep, although I know that won't happen. Every time I close my eyes I see him. Maybe that's not such a bad thing after all.

I groan and roll onto my back. My hands rub the last bit of the dream from my vision as I throw the blankets off. Why is it that every time you want to lie in bed all day, you can't? I don't want to move. I want to spend the day wrapped up in my head with my mystery man.

I drop my feet to the warm hardwood and drag myself to the bathroom to freshen up, before heading to the kitchen to get the coffee brewing. I know I'll seriously need it today, given I missed out on some much needed sleep.

My apartment takes up the entire second story of the building my antique shop is in. I do have a third floor, but it's for storage. After my mom passed away, I moved in here. Her death came around the same time as my divorce from my cheating, asshole of a husband. I had planned on moving in to help care for her, but I didn't have enough time. The cancer took her sooner than expected.

I grew up here, however moved away for college, and then work. My dad is someone I've never met, nor know anything about. My mom always kept the details vague in regards to him, and I don't have any siblings. It was up to me to handle everything for my mom. She left very detailed paperwork of how she wanted her service and burial. Her store instructions were included in there, as well. She was adamant that I take it over. It was nothing I wanted to do. I had a job in advertising, which I quit to run her business. I couldn't let her final wishes fall on deaf ears.

So, here I sit at the table in the eat-in kitchen of my apartment, over the antique store that my mother left me. It's been a year since she died. I've changed out the furniture in the apartment to things that are more my taste, which was a little tough. With every piece I replaced, it was as if I was getting rid of pieces of her. I knew I couldn't continue to live in the past, though.

The items she had fit with her taste, but I like a more contemporary style. Knowing what she would want, I put her pieces in the store for others to purchase. She always said no piece was too old or too worn. There was a home out there for every item in the store, they were only waiting for their owners to show up. She spoke like each piece were a living being. I guess, in a way, they did talk to her. Each had a story, many years of being loved before finding its way to her store.

Most days I'm bored senseless waiting for people to come in. Antiques are an acquired taste. The people who do come in look adoringly over each piece, and I sit and wonder what they see. Maybe the pieces call to them like they did my mom.

I read. A lot. If I didn't, the days would drag on. After I lock up each night, I go back to my apartment and to my sad existence. This is not the way I expected to be spending my time at the age of twenty-three. There hasn't been another man in my life and I'm not actively looking for one. After what I went through with my ex, I'm in no hurry. I'm lonely, though. All of the friends I had from the advertising firm forgot about me when I left, and I'm not one to chase people who don't seem interested in putting in the effort to remain friends.

The sweet sound of coffee dripping into the pot reaches my ears. Grabbing a yogurt from the fridge and some granola, I sit them on the table until the coffee is finished brewing. I'm not big on breakfast, but if I don't eat I'll feel sick all day.

After eating and downing two cups of my much needed caffeine, I go into the bathroom to get ready. I throw on a pair of dark denim jeans and a long-sleeved, black v-neck, then run wet fingers through my long, black hair in an effort to tame some of the frizz. My hair has a natural wave that only needs a little encouragement from the water to become springy. Then I hope for no humidity today.

I apply light makeup to my eyes and call it a day.

I don't need to get all dolled up to sit behind a counter for hours on end. Before I go downstairs, I pour the remainder of the coffee into a travel mug and switch the pot off. This will get me through until lunch when I'll take a short break to refill.

Downstairs, I switch on all of the lights and walk to the front door to turn over the sign saying I'm open, and unlock the door. The store is in the middle of downtown in the tiny rural area I live in. It's your typical country setting of one main street with all of the stores you need on it and nothing else for at least a half hour's drive. The kindness of the people that live here is something I cherish, even if I don't venture out often. When I used to live in the city, people would walk right into you on the street and not even apologize. Being in this small town is a huge change of pace.

One hour goes by. Two. Four. I stand to lock the door so I can refill my cup, when an elderly couple walks in. I smile and sit back down, while they browse the items in the store. Watching them gives me a slight pain in my chest wishing my own grandparents were still alive. I have no family anymore. My mom was all I had left.

They continue their perusal and stop in front of a large, cherry dresser with a tall mirror in the center. The varnish is chipped and the mirror has seen better days. The thing has been here as long as I can remember. No one even looks at it for more than five seconds. The price tag alone turns them away. If it's really worth that much I don't know, but my mom priced it the way she did for a reason, so I leave it alone.

They open it up and take a look at the inside of the drawers. Each one is opened then closed. When they get to the bottom I see them pause while looking inside. Craning my neck, I try to see what they found to cause such intense interest. I haven't opened any of the drawers, so I'm not sure what could be in there. The older man looks my way and I take that as a hint to walk to them.

"Hi," I say in a cheery voice. "Can I help you with something?"

"The drawer doesn't seem right." The woman's eyes wrinkle at the corner while she studies it.

Bending down, my brows furrow and I look inside. She's right. It's like the interior is only half of the depth it should be. Pushing around on the piece of wood at the bottom, I find it gives a little in the back. I continue to press on it until the corner of the wood lifts. When I'm able to pry it free, I notice there is a hidden storage space. Tucked into the corner of the space is a small, pewter box.

I take it in my hand and stand to look it over. The detail is amazing for such a small piece. On the lid are two roses and a sunflower with sweeping lines around the border. It's in the shape of a rectangle with scalloped edges, and each side has roses on it with more filigree work. There are four tiny legs, which give the box a delicate look.

Opening the lid, I notice red velvet inside, which has become worn in spots over time. There is a key within and a folded up piece of paper. I withdraw the key first to study it. It's made of gold and is very ornate. There is a crown on one end with golden swirls around it. The two teeth are shaped like nothing I've ever seen. They are mirror images of one another and covered in tiny golden leaves. It's heavy and cold in my hand. What a beautiful key.

"It's a skeleton key," the man says from beside me. I look up at him and see him studying the items in my hands. He takes the key from my palm and holds it up to the light. "I've never seen one quite like this," he adds.

His wife steps up, lifting her round glasses from her petite nose to look at it as well. While they are studying it, I remove the letter from the box. I'm shocked to see my name in my mother's handwriting on the front. I sit the box down on the dresser and place my hand over my mouth, while tears form in my eyes. I miss her so much, and here in my hand I hold something she left for me.

> *Alison,*
> *If you are reading this letter, that means I wasn't there to give this box to you. I apologize for leaving you to discover this, but it's a secret I must have thought you weren't ready for yet. I know you won't*

believe what you're about to read, but I need you to keep an open mind.

Where we live is not the only place where humans reside. There are other realms out there, too many to count. They are hidden and kept secret. I know this, because I've been to one. I even used to live there. It's a place very different from our world. There are many kingdoms within. Kings and queens, knights, everything you've read about in fairy tales. It really exists and I want you to discover it as well. It's part of who you are.

You see, your father didn't abandon you. I left him while I was pregnant with you. I had no choice. I needed to keep you safe. I'm sorry for never telling you this, but I did what was best at the time. I knew you wouldn't understand until you were older. Please forgive me for holding onto this for so long.

The key in this box opens a door to your father's realm. To find the door, you must go to the back of the closet in my bedroom. Move all of the boxes and clothes aside. On the far right corner, you'll see a handle in the wall. Pull it open and you will reveal the door to their realm.

Ali, before you open this door, know that once you cross over, you might never be able to return. The key has a tendency of *disappearing and reappearing as it sees fit. It's even disappeared out of this box on occasion, but always came back. I think it's waiting for you.*

The key has been around a very long time. If once you cross over you still have the key, then you should be able to come home, but you might not be able to return to the realm. There is no telling when the key will disappear. Also, every time the portal is opened, it allows pieces of our world into theirs. Their way of living is very different than ours. And we don't want the key to get into the wrong hands.

I'm sorry for not telling you this in person. I did what I had to for your safety and theirs. When I left their realm a great war was going on, and I didn't feel it was safe for us. The key appeared and I knew it was a chance I needed to take. I only hope your father's still alive, when and if, you go through the door.

If you decide to go, it will be nothing like you've ever known, but tell whoever you meet that you're the daughter of Rafe Pine. My hope is that whoever you find first will bring you to him. You must be on guard until you are safe with him or his people. Please, be very careful.

I'm sorry I've left you, Ali. I love you more than I could ever express. Take care

and trust in your heart, my daughter. It will
never lead you astray.
Love,
Mom

My mind is left reeling. Could everything she wrote be true? I feel someone shaking me and look up to find the elderly couple before me.

"Dear, are you okay?" the woman asks.

"What? Oh, yes. I'm fine." I quickly fold up the letter and place it back in the box. I see the man is still holding the key and take it from him to put with the letter. If everything my mom said was accurate, then I need to guard this with my life.

They are both looking at me with confusion. I plaster on a fake smile. "I'm sorry, but I need to close."

"We're interested in this dresser," he states.

"I'm sorry. That's no longer for sale." I can't sell it. What if there is more inside?

I usher the irritated couple out of the store, turn the lock, and flip over the sign to "Closed." Rushing back to the dresser, I root through every part of it. I take out the drawers, inspecting each one. I reach inside the frame and make sure I've covered every inch. Nothing else is discovered. The next place I'm going is the bedroom closet.

CHAPTER TWO

Decisions

I run up the stairs, taking them two at a time. I need to find out if what my mother wrote is true. Inside her closet, I shove everything aside. It's one area I hadn't completely gone through. Out of sight, out of mind. I keep saying I'll do it another time, only another time never comes.

When I have all of the boxes out of the way, and the clothes are relocated to the rods on either side, I look over the blank, white wall. Taking out her letter again, I skim it quickly. She said there will be a handle on the right side. There's nothing visible, so I run my hand along the corner where the walls meet. All the way down the sheetrock to the floor I go and then back up, but much slower this time. When I'm about halfway up, I feel a bump in the wall. I use my nail and run it down the side of it. Sure enough, my nail pushes through what feels like paper, and I grasp a handle. Wrapping my fingers over it, I pull firmly on the wall. With a little effort it begins to move. Once I have the wall completely open, I see a door. It looks like any other weathered one. It's a slate blue and the paint is chipping. I would think it's been out weathering storms with the way it appears. There's a piece of wrought iron crossing it in the middle, leading to a lock and knob in the same color as the wood.

The hidden wall is real. The door, leading to who knows where, is real. I bend at the waist and start to hyperventilate. How is all of this possible, and I never knew? I have more questions than answers, and there is no one here to answer them for me. The next question is, do I want to go through it? She wasn't lying, at least not so far. I can't even wrap my head around that there could be a whole other world just beyond that door.

I sit on the floor once my breathing steadies and stare at the door for hours. I read the letter again. My mother was always down to earth, never an airhead. This could be real, not a wild goose chase. Although, why she would send me on some off the wall adventure, I don't know. That leads me to believe it's not a fairy tale. I could meet my father on the other side. If he's still alive.

The longer I sit here, the more I want to go through. If I go through, I might not be able to come back. She said the key might disappear. What the hell kind of key is this anyway? How does something inanimate disappear?

I have to be sure I really want to see the other side. I also can't disregard the thought that once I'm there, I might not want to leave. Although, what if they're still at war? I'm going to sleep on it. Yes, that's the smart thing to do.

I eat dinner and go back to stare at the door. Watch television, door. Brush my teeth, door. I keep waiting for something to happen or someone to come crashing through. Shaking my head, I climb into bed.

An hour goes by and I'm still awake. I pick up the book I've been reading and flip the bedside lamp on. Two hours later and my eyes are finally starting to close. Then I enter my dreamland again.

It's the same as it was the night before, and all of the other times, except for two things. The cottage doesn't disappear when I emerge from it, and the man on the hill is pointing toward the door. The same door, I realize, as the one inside my closet.

The door is weathered, but what surrounds it is beautiful. It's the same ivy I've seen before, but it's brighter now, with beautiful hues of pink, purple, teal, and even the azure color of the flowers I usually see. The only things it doesn't completely cover are the windows and door.

My gaze bounces back and forth between the man and the cottage. He seems insistent that I need to go to the door by the way his hand keeps pointing at it, which doesn't make sense since I just came through it. His dragon is rearing up, front legs off the ground as it kicks toward the sky. It's angry, I can sense it. What's going on? I need to get to him, no matter what he's pointing at. As I start to run, the dream fades.

I wake with a start and immediately go to the closet. Flipping on the light within, I walk to the wooden door and run my fingers over it. My decision is made; I'm going through.

The clock by the bed reads four in the morning. The sky is dark, except for the occasional strike of lightning, and I can hear thunder in the distance. I change into a pair of jeans and a black t-shirt with lace on the edges of the sleeves. It's the first one I find. In every dream I feel comfortable with regard to the weather. Just in case, I grab a backpack. Who knows how long I'll be gone? Sweatshirt, change of clothes, extra bra, panties, and socks. I also pack some protein bars and a few bottles of water. I even shove a small pocket knife inside, just in case.

Walking through the apartment, I make sure all of the lights are off and the door is locked. I know I locked up the store before I came upstairs yesterday. I highly doubt anyone will try to break into my place, but you never know. In reality, I'd be surprised if anyone notices when I don't open the store today. I have no real friends here. There's no one to miss me. This thought helps solidify my decision.

I find the new pair of sneakers I bought a few weeks ago and put them on. For all I know I'm really going to have to run when I get to the other side. With the bag thrown over my shoulder, I pick up the pewter box and withdraw the gold skeleton key. I don't want to leave the box and letter behind, so I slip it into the bag.

Standing in the doorway of the closet, I take a few deep breaths. At the last minute, I grab the framed picture of my mom I keep on my dresser. Tucking it gently inside the bag amongst my clothes, I finally feel ready to leave this world behind.

In a few long strides I'm in front of the door. I reach out with a shaky hand and insert the key into the lock. With a gentle turn, I hear a click. I don't want anyone to follow me and pull the wall closed when I open the door. I take one step out the door and bring the wall completely shut behind me. Once I'm fully through, I retrieve the key and the door closes on its own with a whoosh. I note that the key is still in my hand and place it in my pocket. I can go home if I want to. It didn't disappear yet, anyway.

I'm almost nervous to turn around. What if what I find looks nothing like my dreams? What if I made a huge mistake? What if the realm doesn't exist and I'm standing on a ledge outside of my own apartment? I watch too many movies.

Closing my eyes, I turn and feel the sun against my skin. That's a good sign. The sun is always shining in my dreams and it was dark when I left home. I open my eyes and before me is the field of azure flowers. Lifting my hand to block out some of the sun, I notice the flowers go on for as far as I can see. I'm here. I'm really here.

Looking behind me, I see the cottage covered with vibrant ivy. I can't believe this. I pinch myself to make sure it's real.

"Ouch!" I call out. Maybe that wasn't the smartest move.

I take hesitant steps and adjust my pack to rest evenly on my back. In front of me, in the distance, is the hill, but there is no man or dragon on it. I look around and realize that the cottage is at the edge of a forest line. There are dense trees behind me and the sunny field in front. Not wanting to go into the dark forest, I step forward into the field.

The miniature blue sunflowers brush against my jeans as I walk. Their brilliant color makes me smile as I remember seeing them in my sleep. I even bend down to touch them to make sure they feel the same. Silky, just as I recall. If the man were here, it would be better than the dream, because I know I won't wake up soon. This is my new reality. Another realm, but reality all the same. Looking back, I notice the cottage still stands. It hasn't disappeared like in so many of my dreams.

I hear a shout in the distance. Looking around, I don't see anyone, only the forest and the azure field. I move further into the flowers, scanning the area as

I go. Then I feel the ground shake. First it starts off as a gentle vibration moving from my feet up into my legs, but soon becomes a full on rumble. The ground is moving to the point that I'm having a hard time standing.

I'm too busy trying to maintain my balance to notice the men on horses charging toward me, until they are rushing past as if I'm invisible. I scream out and cover my head with my arms in an effort to protect myself.

There are so many of them. When it finally seems like they have all gone past, I put my arms back by my sides and watch the large group charge toward the forest. Then I hear a voice. A deep masculine voice.

"Are you lost?"

I turn around and see a man on top of a beautiful black horse. He's wearing a long-sleeved, black shirt with matching black pants and boots. Do I know him? It's more of a feeling than a recognition. I think he's the man from my dreams. No, I never saw him close up, but I know the way he made me feel when I was running toward him. I know deep within, this is him.

He seems to be studying me as well. With wide eyes, he asks on a whisper, "Is it really you?"

"I'm sorry?"

"You're her. The woman from my dreams. I can't believe it!" He drops down from the stallion with ease and steps until we are almost toe-to-toe.

"You...dreamt...about me?" Could he really have been dreaming about me like I have of him?

"Yes, it's the craziest thing. Every night you were in my dreams. Except Tali was always by my side. And we were never this close. Always a distance away." He lifts his chin toward the hill.

"Tali?" I ask.

"My dragon, of course."

"Of course." Sure. Tali. He says it like I should have already known it. As if dragons are common place.

"Where is Tali?" I ask while scanning the skies.

"She's back at the castle. Today is a hunting day so she wasn't needed."

This has got to be the weirdest conversation I've ever had. You don't need dragons on hunting days. You use horses. Yup, I knew that.

"What were you hunting?" I inquire.

"A fix."

"A fix? Do you mean a fox?"

"No, fix. It's a small creature with red fur and green eyes and a short, stubby tail." He cocks his head to the side. "You've never seen one before?" I shake my head.

Then the ground starts rumbling again. A flash of

red comes at us, and I instinctively move closer to the man. The animal stops a few feet from us. It's the oddest looking creature. The face of a house cat, but the body of a fox minus the tail. Its eyes are a bright, emerald green, and then it's gone, off with speed that could rival a cheetah.

"That was a fix."

"I've never seen anything like it. Why are you hunting it?"

"You haven't?" He must think I'm from here. "He keeps stealing the fruit that our people work so hard to grow, so we decided to hunt him down. It's been quiet lately, so I thought it would be fun to get my men out. We're making a sport of it."

The vibration strengthens, but this time I know what's coming. I step even closer. I'm only a few inches from him now.

"Don't be afraid," he murmurs against my ear. "My men won't harm you. You're safe with me."

The men and horses rush past us, leaving my hair blowing around my face. Surprisingly, the man's horse doesn't move as the others race by. I can't imagine them catching the fix as fast as it is. I gaze up at the man by my side and get a good look at him. He's got dark brown hair and light blue eyes. He has a mustache and beard that are trimmed short. He must feel my eyes on him, because he turns to look at me.

I'm on the taller side and tend to shy away from

dating men shorter than me. My ex-husband was about even with my height. The man before me is a few inches taller, which I appreciate.

"What's your name?" he asks.

"Alison Wescot."

He smiles and I notice his straight, white teeth. "I'm Lucas Azure. Tell me, why have I only seen you in my dreams and never in my kingdom?"

"I've never been here before. Well, not really. I've dreamt of this place, and you."

His eyes widen slightly. "You have?"

Nodding, I add, "I only just came through the door."

"The door?" he asks.

"Yes, the door to the cottage." I turn and point to the slate blue door on the ivy covered structure.

"You live in the run-down cottage?"

"No," I smile, shaking my head. "I'm from another place. When I went through that door, I appeared here."

"That's impossible." He walks to the cottage in long strides and opens the door. Stepping inside, he's only gone for a few seconds before he returns. "There's nothing in there but some broken furniture, cobwebs, and a lot of dust."

"Maybe to get through you need the key," I mumble, thinking to myself.

"What's that?" he calls.

"Oh, nothing." I decide to keep the key to myself for the moment. Besides, what if he takes it from me, and I can't ever go home?

He comes to stand before me again. "Come, I'll take you to my home," he says with an extended hand.

As much as I want to go with him, I need to find my father. Plus, I don't know him. "I'm actually looking for someone."

"Who?" he asks tightly. His body tenses, his shoulders square.

"My father. Could you help me find him?"

I watch him visibly relax. Was he jealous? He doesn't know anything about me, but then again I do feel this strange connection to him that I don't want to analyze at the moment.

"If you've never been here before, how do you have a father here?"

"It's a long story. One I can explain, but I'm really hoping my father is alive and I can meet him."

"What's his name?"

"Rafe Pine."

With wide eyes, Lucas takes a few steps back. "That can't be," he stammers.

"What? Is he dead?" I'm starting to tremble. Did I make a huge mistake? What if I went through the door only to find out he's gone?

"No, he's alive." I let out a breath and relax. "But you can't be his daughter. You look nothing like him."

"I'm a mirror image of my mother. Everyone used to always say that we could be sisters."

"Your mother?" He looks at me like he's trying to piece things together.

"Yes, I look just like my mother."

"What was her name?"

"Eliza."

His face hardens as does his voice. "I need you to come with me. Now."

CHAPTER THREE

Revelations

I don't like the look on his face and start to retreat from him. What happened to the kind, warm man? He's faster than me. The second I turn to run, he grips my arm and pulls me toward his horse. His fingers bite into my skin. Maybe he's not the man I was hoping he'd be.

Attempting to wrench my arm free, I hiss, "I'm not going anywhere with you. Let me go!"

"We can do this two ways, Alison. Either you come with me of your own will, or I make you. But either way, you will get on that horse."

"Why are you doing this? I didn't do anything wrong," I cry.

He halts in his tracks and turns to seethe his

words at me. "You might not have, but your father did. He's a murderer. He killed my best friend in battle."

His words rock me to my core. My father is a murderer? How can this be? My mom would have never been with someone so vicious. She didn't have a mean bone in her body.

I'm trying to figure out a reason why he would have killed someone so important. "Maybe he didn't know he was so important to you."

"He knew. Make no mistake. I saw his face after he did it."

Tears are threatening to spill from my eyes. "I don't even know him."

We are right next to his horse. "Get on, Alison." Some of the anger has left his voice, and if I'm not mistaken, there is indecision in his eyes.

There is no use in fighting him. He's bigger and stronger than me. At least if I move on my own, maybe he won't hurt me.

I look up and take in the size of the steed in front of me. He's tall. Way too tall. "I've never ridden a horse and he's too big. I can't climb onto him."

Lucas grabs my hips, and with an effortless ease, lifts me up in the air, so I can grab the saddle and pull myself the rest of the way up. He swiftly climbs up and settles himself behind me with my bag between us.

In my ear he says, "Don't try anything." What does he think I'm going to do? Launch myself from this height and break a leg? I'm not jumping down. Yeah, I want to run, but that chance is gone for the time being.

We start a slow trot in the opposite direction of the cottage. I have a sinking feeling in my stomach. I wanted to come here. I thought I'd find my very own knight and live out some beautiful fairy tale. The opposite is happening. I found a knight, but one whose friend died at the hands of my father. Now I'm being taken to who knows where and my knight is no longer friendly.

The further we go, the fewer pretty blue flowers I see. We start climbing a steep hill, and once at the top, I can see a castle. There is a great, grey stone wall surrounding it, and in the middle is a tall, weathered red tower house. The windows along the sides are arched at the top. There are other structures within the wall that are the same color as the tower house, including a circular building; which isn't as tall as the tower, but still massive with square windows. The closer we get, I realize that the castle is surrounded by water with a stone bridge connecting it with the land. At the top of the tower house is a large flag, which appears to be the same azure color as the flowers with an eagle on it. The eagle's wings are spread wide.

"Is that where you're taking me?" I ask, inclining my chin to the castle.

"Yes, that's my home and where you'll be staying until I can contact King Pine."

I turn abruptly and come face-to-face with Lucas. His breath mingles with my own and my heart seems to stop in the moment. His eyes move from mine down to my lips. Instinctively I lick my bottom lip. His own part and we are again looking into each other's eyes. My body is starting to react to his. I can feel heat spread throughout me. The horse slows suddenly, effectively breaking us from the spell.

Facing forward again, I say, "I didn't know my father is a king. My mother is no longer alive, and I only have a letter from her telling me very little about this world."

"This world?"

"Yeah, the one you live in. I told you I wasn't from here."

"Yes, but I thought you were from another kingdom."

"No, Lucas. I'm from another place entirely. I told you the door brought me here. I left my apartment and appeared here."

"That's not possible. I don't believe you. I went into the cottage. There's nothing there."

I wave a hand dismissively. "Believe what you want, but I'm telling the truth."

He scoffs behind me. "I'm reluctant to believe anything you say due to your relation to King Pine."

"He's your enemy?"

"Yes."

"So you have your own king?" I'm so confused and trying to figure out everything about where I am. Knowledge is power, right?

"Yes, my father is King Azure."

"You're a prince?" I ask in astonishment.

"Yes, but I'm not next in line for the throne. I'm the youngest of four and have no desire to rule this land. I'm happy defending it."

"Are you a warrior?"

"Yes, in a manner of speaking. I have a small, elite group, who defend this territory with our lives. We have a larger army that I'm in charge of as well, but only use them when we are at war or to stand guard around the castle. They all report to me." When he talks about his place and his men, I can tell how proud he is of it; how much it means to him.

We are closing in on the castle when a loud roar reaches my ears. Then I see five dragons take to the air just beyond the tower house. They look like they're playing with one another. Nipping at each other, chasing, they remind me of the way dogs play. There is always one dominant that puts the others in their place. With the dragons, that appears to be the white one.

"Is that your dragon?" I ask pointing to the sky.

"Yes, that's Tali."

"Do they always play like that?"

"When they can. It's a nice way for them to enjoy themselves. When we need them, they're always ready to go, and we work them hard. When we don't, we tend to let them do as they please. They always stay near the castle. Even at night they stay in their own area."

"Are people attacking you often?"

"Why are you asking so many questions?"

I shrug. "I'm curious by nature, and I've never seen a dragon in real life before, nor a castle. This is all new to me." He doesn't need to know I'm banking every piece of information in my head to use later.

He slows the horse to a walk and asks, "You're being honest with me, aren't you?" He must really think I want to sit here and lie to him. That I'm making everything up. I'm not after anything except to protect myself.

"I have no reason to lie."

"Yes, you do. You're the daughter of King Pine. That alone is enough to make you lie."

I turn to peer at him over my shoulder. In a gentle, placating voice, I say, "Lucas, I have never met my father and didn't even know who he was until yesterday. I come here, and you tell me he is a murderer. I'm not exactly feeling all warm and fuzzy where he's concerned. Would I like to know more about him? Yes, but only because he's my father. Right now, I don't have any desire to be in his presence, if what you are saying is true. I don't want to go to a man that's cruel."

He tenses behind me. I'm not sure why, since I wasn't speaking of him. He still doesn't believe me, though. "I find it hard to believe you know nothing of our kingdoms or the wars we have battled. Who are our enemies and who are our allies? Your father is a vicious, brutal killer, Alison. He killed Leo and countless others during battle."

"Can you stop the horse for a minute?"

"Why?"

I roll my eyes. Seriously, I'm sitting here with no weapons, and in a fight with him I wouldn't stand a chance. This is crazy. "I want to show you something. Proof that I'm telling you the truth." If he doesn't trust the fact that I knew nothing of my father, I wonder what will happen to me when we get to the castle. Will I be locked up inside? Will I be sent away to the man I don't know, but am of blood relation to? And what will he do with me? He's never met me. I could be treated awfully for all I know.

Lucas stops the horse and I reach around to my backpack. "What are you doing?" he inquires with narrow eyes.

"What I need to show you is in my bag."

"Then I'll get it." Eye roll number two. Does he honestly think I'm carrying a gun or something? If I was, I would have used it by now to not get dragged away.

"Fine. Inside my bag is a pewter box. Inside is a letter. Read it."

I feel him rummaging through my bag and wait for him to find what I said. Then I remember I put a knife in there. I hope he doesn't find it. I'll really be considered a threat then. Even if it is only a pocket knife. Next I hear the crumpling noise of paper being unfolded. I sit and wait for him to read it. I watch the sky and the dragons, who are still playing in the air.

His voice is low, but I can hear the surprise in it that he might finally believe me. "You only found this yesterday?"

"Yes. I couldn't believe it when I first read it, but everything she said is true so far."

"Where are you from?"

"A small country town in the United States."

"The United States? Where's that?" I wonder how many of the people who live here even know another realm exists outside of their own. The same with where I live. Does anyone else know about this place?

"It's the country I live in. You've never met anyone from another realm?"

"Another realm? No, I didn't know any other place existed. I only thought it was the kingdoms we have here, in our country. Yes, there are other kingdoms far away, across oceans even, but this is all I knew. I can't believe this. There's a portal in the cottage. Amazing."

"I didn't know either until I walked through that door and into the field of blue flowers that I've been dreaming about."

He tucks everything back into my bag. I hear the zipper slide closed before we start moving again.

Lucas lets out a deep breath. "I don't know what's going to happen when we reach the castle."

I don't turn around, but place my hand on his leg nestled next to mine. "I'm scared." That's the honest truth. There are so many things that could happen, and that's only in my imagination. This is a world I know nothing of, or their ways when dealing with someone like me. I'm the daughter of the enemy and not just any enemy, a king.

"I'm going to be honest with you, Alison. When we go over that bridge, everyone is going to wonder where you came from and who you are. You don't dress the same as our women. Most of them wear long skirts or dresses. Only women who hold higher roles within our kingdom dress differently. People with magical abilities like seers or royals.

"When my father finds out who you're related to, you're going to be locked up. You will be seen as a spy, sent here to learn about our defenses. I'm going to have to talk with him and explain everything. I'll need to show him the letter. He isn't going to believe me otherwise. It's the only evidence I'll have at my disposal."

Ice spreads through my body at the thought of being locked up. I'm not a spy. They aren't going to believe him. I just know it. I shouldn't have come. I could still be safe in my apartment.

I'm so lost in my own thoughts that I don't realize we are only feet away from the castle. The horse takes it first steps on the grey and white stone bridge. Its hooves clop along as we approach the tall, imposing doors.

Two guards stand on either side in armor similar to what I saw Lucas wear in my dreams. These have the eagle on them, with its wings spread wide, and talons showing in the same steel blue color. On the top of the wall, I notice other guards patrolling. My heart starts to pound in my chest. I don't want to go in. What if I never come out?

I twist my body and look at Lucas with pleading eyes. "Please don't take me in there. They aren't going to believe me. I don't want to be locked up. Please." Tears start falling onto my cheeks. I'm unable to hold them back.

He stops the horse just a few feet from the doors. With a gentle hand he reaches up and captures my tears with this fingers. "Shhh, don't cry. I won't let them hurt you. You might get locked up, but only until I can clear things up with my father. Be brave, my princess. I'll protect you."

"You said you were going to contact King Pine about me. What changed? Why do you want to protect me now?"

"I believe you. That is what's changed. I can't be too careful. You must understand that. I find a woman in the middle of a field, who happens to be the daughter of our enemy. Now that I have proof of your words, it eases my mind. I also saw the knife in your bag and knew if you wanted to harm me you would have. It's in my pocket now, by the way. Plus, I use my instincts a lot and they tell me I can trust you. They tell me more, but that is for me to know right now. I feel like I've known you much longer than I have. Seeing you for so long in my dreams, I can't explain it, but there's something very special about you."

His words cause my body to relax marginally. They are what I need to hear. I might be in a cell once we get inside, but Lucas would watch over me, right? He said he'd protect me. I only hope he means it. I close my eyes and lean into his touch, relishing this moment which will soon break. I've been alone for too long. It's nice to have someone touch me and care.

Heavy footsteps come toward us. His hand drops from my face, and I immediately miss the warmth of his skin on mine.

"Prince Lucas," one of the guards calls. "Allow me to walk you in." Lucas nods as the man takes the reins and walks the horse with us on it through the door. The other guard remains at his station, but bows as we pass.

Once inside, I'm amazed by all I see. The courtyard is covered with the same grey and white stone that the bridge is. There are a few vendors within the walls with colorful carts selling different goods. There are azure colored flags sticking out from the wall with the same eagle on them, with its talons spread wide and feathers sticking out on either side.

Men bow and women curtsy as we pass by, and Lucas nods in their direction. I notice the men are dressed in loose fitting twill pants with long-sleeved cotton shirts. The women are wearing dresses or skirts that reach their feet. Some are more colorful than others. Aren't they warm? I only just got here, but sweat has formed on my brow from the sun. It's not stifling, just warm.

We attract everyone's stares as we make our way through the courtyard. I don't look like these women, with my fitted top and jeans that form to my hips and legs. I wonder what they think of me. A couple of people even whisper as we pass by. Lifting my head, I focus straight ahead and not on those around us.

The horse is brought to a halt in front of the tower house. Lucas dismounts first, then helps me down. He thanks the guard who escorted us in and leads me into a dark room.

CHAPTER FOUR

Neighbor

Lucas said he would protect me, that no one would harm me. I can't help but feel he won't be able to keep his word. Sure, he's a prince, but he's not the king. I'm sure the king makes the final decisions, and I'll be labeled as a spy. Even as I reflect back on how I appeared and what I said, it seems so far-fetched. Without the letter I'd really be screwed.

My body is trembling. Lucas stops, and I bump into him with my shoulder, since I'm not paying attention. I look around waiting for something to happen, unsure why we halted.

We're in a dark hallway with only bits of light filtering in through windows. There were a handful of guards we passed, but now we're alone. He turns to me and speaks in a soft voice. "Alison, I can feel you shaking. Please, be calm. I already told you I'd watch over you. You must trust me."

My voice is barely above a whisper. "But I don't even know you."

His head tilts slightly to the side. "Don't you? We've been meeting in our dreams for a while now. Have you ever felt frightened of me or worried?"

"No, not frightened of you. Worried, yes. Scared in general, yes. I always felt like something was about to happen to me, and I needed to get to you; that I would be safe by your side."

"And now? Are you afraid of me? Do you think I'll let harm befall you?"

"I'm still not frightened of you, but I don't think you'll have the last say as to my fate. I think the king's word will be final."

He shakes his head. His dark brown hair that was swept back falls onto his forehead. I have to resist the urge to brush it back. "Have faith in me," he urges.

I look away. I can't have faith in someone I don't know. No matter how many times I've seen him while asleep, I don't actually know him well enough to put all of my trust in. Although, what choice do I have? No one else is going to sweep in and save me. The only person who I'm related to in this realm doesn't even know I'm here. Does he even know I exist? I was born in the U.S., at least that's what my birth certificate says. Who knows what's true and what's not anymore? Only two people know the answers and one is gone.

"Ali, believe in me." I nod. It's all I can do. To speak a confirmation out loud would be a lie.

To my surprise, he takes my hand in his and leads me through the corridor. I have so many conflicting emotions where he's concerned. He's shown me he can be hard one moment and soft the next. We stop outside a grand wooden door with thin pieces of wrought iron curling in design over it. It's closed and guards are stationed on either side. They both bow to Lucas.

"Is my father in?" he asks.

"Yes, Your Highness."

Lucas nods and steps toward the door. One of the guards opens it so we may pass through. The door shuts with a loud clang, making me jump. There is a gorgeous chandelier above the long table before us. It's wrought iron with candles atop it. Three men are sitting at the far end. One at the head and one on either side. The man at the head I know is the king. He has the same color hair as Lucas, but is stockier with a full beard. He exudes power. None of the men are dressed formally, only in simple cotton, navy long-sleeved shirts and black pants. The king's eyes immediately fall on me and he tries to hide a gasp, but I hear his sharp intake of breath. Next, they are on our joined hands, then to his son. The men at his sides shift in their chairs to look at us as well.

"Son," he says stiffly. "Who have you brought us?"

"Father, this is Alison Wescot. She's new to our area. I need to speak with you about her. Alone." The last word is edged in steel. The two men next to the king look to their leader, who nods and they stand to leave. But as they go, they give Lucas nasty glares. In turn, I see his face harden and know he saw them. There is hatred between these men. That much is evident.

"Come," the king says. "Have a seat and bring your friend with you."

Lucas walks to the chair beside his father. He squeezes my hand and offers me a small smile before pulling out a chair for me. We both sit. There are no other people in the room. Only the three of us, no guards.

"What is so important that you had to kick Evan and Levi out?"

"I need you to promise me two things before I tell you. One, you cannot speak or react until I'm finished. Two, you agree to sit here and discuss everything with an open mind."

"Lucas," the king warns.

"Father, please. Hear me out."

He sighs. "Fine." He waves his hand toward Lucas, motioning him to speak.

"I found Alison by the woods. She walked

through the door of the old cottage into our kingdom, but she's not from here. She's from a whole other place that I never knew existed until I met her today."

The king's eyes widen then narrow quickly. He leans forward on the table and directs his next words to me. "Where are you from?"

I shift nervously in my seat and fold my hands in my lap. "A small town in middle of Colorado. In the United States."

"Near the Rocky Mountains?" Um, what? How does he know what and where the Rocky Mountains are?

"I'm sorry?" I ask timidly.

"You heard me."

"Yes, sir." Sir? Where did that come from? Was that the right way to address him? Hell if I know.

"Father, you've heard of the area she's from?" Lucas asks surprisingly.

"Yes."

"What? How? And why haven't I been told?"

"You don't need to know everything. Not right now at least. There are some things better kept quiet. I highly suggest you keep this information between the three of us."

"Of course."

"Now, what else do you have to tell me, my son?

Because I know this isn't all of it. There has to be more." The king watches me like a hawk. He's taking in every part of my face, waiting for me to say something. The question is what? I have nothing to offer him.

"Yes, there is. I'm going to give you a letter to read, but you must know that Ali only read it yesterday. She knew nothing before that. You must remember that." The king nods and extends his hand for the letter. Lucas looks to me and I fumble with the bag still on my back. Have I really been sitting in this chair with this thing behind me and not realized it? Must be my nerves.

I quickly reach behind me and unzip my bag. I withdraw the pewter box and sit it on the table. An audible gasp comes from the king. I look up and see his mouth is open; he's fixated on the box.

"Where did you get that?" he asks shakily.

"My mother. She left it for me."

"Give me the letter and whatever else is in the box." His words are hard and make me afraid to hand it over, but I know I must.

"There's nothing else inside." I'm not telling him I still have the key. Obviously this box is significant to him somehow. I wonder why, though. He'll know I had the key once he reads it, but he won't know I still do.

I place the letter in Lucas' hand who gives it to the king. The king's lips go into a thin line as he reads it. His hand tightens causing the paper to crinkle. Then he slams his fist down on the table and throws daggers at me with his eyes. "Guards!" he calls. The two men that are stationed outside of the door come rushing in. "Seize her," he commands. "Take that bag off of her and put her in the dungeon."

"No!" I cry. "Please. You promised. You didn't hear us out."

"You're right. And I won't hear you out. I will hear my son. Without you in the room. Take her away!"

My eyes fly to Lucas, silently pleading for him to do something. He stands, ready to fight, but his father speaks. "If you want her to live, you will sit down, Son."

Lucas' hands fist by his sides and know it's with great effort that he complies. His body is rigid, but he manages to mouth, "It's okay," and watches me being escorted from the room.

I don't go easy. I'm trying to free my arms, using all of my strength, even though it's of no use. I keep trying to plant my feet on the stone floor, but I'm overpowered and now being dragged through the building.

I'm not paying any attention to where they're taking me. I'm too busy squirming, trying to get free, not wanting to give up without a fight. I'm taken down a long, spiral set of stairs into a basement. There is a long hallway with cells on either side. A man with a set of keys is walking in front of us. I only see one other person locked up, and that is right next to the open door I'm being shoved through.

I continue to yell. I know it serves no purpose. Lucas is up there right now, pleading my case. Telling the king I'm not a bad person hopefully, and that I didn't even know who my father was until a day ago. I hope he believes him and I don't have to stay down here for too long.

After the guards walk away, I look around my cell. There are bars in front of me and stone walls on three sides. It smells of dampness and mildew. There is a dark green cot on one side with a grungy looking pillow atop it. There's also a toilet and a sink that I don't even want to think about using right now. It's a good thing I haven't drank anything in hours. I doubt there's enough toilet paper in the world to cover that seat. Hovering wouldn't even be good enough.

I stand in the center of room not wanting to touch a thing. I don't move, but then I see something scurry in front of me and scream, while jumping into the air. Great, filth and rodents, as if the dank smell didn't complete the ambiance on its own.

"Are you okay?" asks a concerned male voice. I'm assuming it's the man who is being kept beside me.

"Peachy!" I shout back. What did he think I was going to say? Oh yeah, I'm fantastic. This is a dream come true!

"You don't look like you belong down here."

"How would you know how I look? You saw me for all of three seconds." I'm snapping at him and don't care. I don't want to make idle chitchat. I want to get the hell out of here.

"I saw you long enough to know you're not from here." No shit.

"What tipped you off?" Yup, I'm in full on bitch mode now. Being locked in a dungeon will do that to me.

He chuckles. "Easy, beautiful one. I mean no harm."

I cross my arms over my chest. "Harm or not, I'm in no mood to talk to you about how I look."

"Do you want to talk about how I know who you are?" My eyes go wide and my lips part. How does he know me? I just got here.

"How could you possibly know who I am?" I inquire, trying not to sound nervous, but my voice still comes out with a quiver.

"I know, because you look exactly like Prince Reid. I'm assuming he's your brother."

I try to speak, but end up choking on my own saliva. I'm gasping in breaths, failing at maintaining my composure. If this guy was unsure if I believed him before, he certainly knows I do now.

"Are you okay?"

"Yup. Fantastic," I rasp. "Need a minute."

I'm bent over at the waist trying to pull air in, while my mind runs with the fact that I have a brother. He could be wrong, right? I'm sure there are a lot of people here who have black hair and blue eyes. That's got to be common.

Standing upright again, I say, "Okay, I'm good. Now, tell me who Prince Reid is."

"You must have only just arrived here. Prince Reid is King Pine's only son." Well, now the odds are definitely in favor of the fact that I have a brother. I am the king's daughter. You'd think my mom would have mentioned this in her letter. How could she leave such a vital detail out? I mean, I have a brother! That's huge!

"How do you know the king?"

"I'm the leader of his army. Allow me to introduce myself. My name is Oliver Sage, and I will protect you, Princess."

CHAPTER FIVE

Promises

"And how do you propose to protect me when you're locked in the cell next to mine?"

"Don't you worry about that," he says dismissively.

"I already have a prince upstairs trying to convince his father to free me. At least he's on the right side of the bars."

"That prince," he spits, "is just as ruthless as his father. That prince will not watch over you. If anything, he will use you as leverage to get what he wants. Now he's in possession of King Pine's top fighter and his only daughter. Your prince is only pretending to have your best interests at heart." He pauses for a beat. "Which one of King Azure's sons is he?"

"Lucas," I say softly. Could all he's saying be true? Am I leverage in the battle between kings?

"Ah, the most vicious of the bunch. I've seen him slit the throat of a man before. There was no hesitation. He killed him and moved on to the next person."

My hand flies to my mouth. I have a hard time believing that the Lucas I met could do such a thing, but I don't really know him. He did say he is part of an elite team who protects their kingdom. I haven't seen the ruthless side of him yet, and after hearing this, I don't want to.

Oliver's voice interrupts my thoughts. "What's your name?"

My voice trembles. "Alison. Alison Wescot."

"Alison, that is not your true last name."

"It is as far as I'm concerned. I wasn't raised here, nor have I ever met my father. Wescot is my name and will remain so."

"As you wish."

We stop talking. I honestly don't know who to believe or who to trust at this point. My mom said to find King Pine, but after Lucas telling me that he killed his best friend, I'm not sure I want to meet him. Now I hear that there's blood on Lucas' hands as well. What the hell goes on in this place? Are they always at war with one another? I need a history lesson and a biography on everyone here. I'm so far out of my element.

Time passes. I'm not sure how much. My legs begin to ache, however the thought of sitting on the cot makes my stomach turn. As I start scanning the floor to see if there is a less grungy spot, I hear voices and the sound of keys clanging.

Perking up, I walk to the bars, my hands grip the cold metal. Something flakes off on my palm. Great, I'll probably get tetanus now.

"Princess, get back," Oliver whispers harshly. "Stay away from the bars." I roll my eyes. Seriously, what the hell is he going to do for me while he's locked up? Reach through the bars and swat at people?

Three men stop in front of me. One is Lucas. "Release her," he commands.

"If you release her, then you must release me as well," demands Oliver.

I notice Lucas' lip curl up on one side. "Oliver Sage, I suggest you keep your mouth shut," he hisses.

"She's not yours, Luke. She belongs with the Pine family."

Lucas moves from my view to stand before him. "Listen to me closely, Sage. The princess is under my guard, not yours. She does not belong to you."

"She belongs to me more than she does to you," Oliver sneers.

"Release her!" Lucas bellows.

The guard with the keys quickly steps up and unlocks my door. I bolt out of it, not wanting to spend another moment in that disgusting space. Lucas is there to catch me, when I trip over a lip in the stone floor in my haste to leave. His strong arms wrap around me, and I can feel his cheek on the top of my head. I don't want to move away. No matter what Oliver said, there is good in this man holding me. I know it.

Oliver yells from his space still behind bars, "Get your hands off of her, Azure! I'm warning you!"

Lucas turns his head, but doesn't release me. I shift slightly in his arms to take in Oliver. He's young, younger than I expected. Maybe around thirty, if I had to guess. He has dirty blond hair and a few days' worth of facial hair. His eyes are a hypnotizing green. I look over the rest of him. His lips are in a thin line, his jaw is set hard, the muscles in his arm are bulging due to the grip he has on the bars. He's attractive. Very attractive, in fact, even in his clothes that look like he's been sleeping on the cot in the cell. Blotches of dirt are scattered over his knees and elbows.

"Do you think I'm scared of you?" he asks Oliver. "You, the grand leader of the Pine Army, rotting in a dungeon in my kingdom. Great job getting captured, by the way."

I can see the pure hatred in Oliver's eyes. "You know she belongs with me!"

Lucas gently releases me and places his body between Oliver and I. "Yours? How can she be yours when you've never met her before today? How can she be yours when she didn't even know you existed until she was placed down here? You know nothing of her," he seethes.

"And you know nothing either, because if you did then you'd know that she was promised to me by her father. He said his first daughter's hand would be mine. You'd know that I've waited my entire life to meet her." Oliver's eyes turn toward me and soften. "Princess Alison, please, don't go with him. I'm yours and will protect you with my life. I need you to stay with me for your safety."

My mouth hangs agape. I'm promised to him? What kind of place did I step into? I'm not going to be forced to spend my life with someone I don't even know. This revelation makes me want to get as far away from Oliver as possible. I need air. I need to get out of this dreary space.

Looking up at Lucas, I plead, "Take me out of here."

"No!" Oliver shouts. "You mustn't leave with him! Princess!"

I ignore his calls and walk with Lucas and the guards out of the dungeon. I can hear him yelling for me all the way up the stairs. We don't stop when we reach the top; we keep moving until we're outside, and I can feel the sun warm my skin. I close my eyes and tilt my head toward the sky. I've never been so happy to be outside before.

There's a gentle tug on my hand, and I open my eyes to see Lucas gesturing for me to follow him. With one foot in front of the other, I move forward. He places an arm around my shoulders and whispers into my ear, "We need to talk, but not here. There are too many ears, which would love nothing more than to get a piece of gossip. Although, I'm guessing they will be gossiping about us anyway."

Looking around, I notice all eyes are on us. People are still in the courtyard, packing up their goods for the day. I duck my head into his shoulder and try not to think about everyone watching me. The further we walk, the fewer people we see. Eventually we stop in front of an ordinary looking, wooden door attached to a small building made of the same weathered red stone as the other structures.

"This is my home," Lucas says. He opens the door and gestures for me to go in first. I take a few hesitant steps inside and wonder if I'm doing the right thing. Should I be in here with him? Alone? Maybe I should insist he take me back to the cottage. I don't know for sure I want to leave him behind, but too many things have happened since I stepped through that door, and not all for the better.

I turn to him, "I need to know what happened with your father. What did he say?"

He scrubs a hand over his face and shuts the door behind him. "We fought. Loudly. He insisted on keeping you down in the dungeon until he could arrange a trade with King Pine. He's keeping something from me, but avoided me when I brought it up."

"A trade?"

He nods. "King Pine is holding two of our men. My father wants to trade you and Sage for them. He also wants to use you to get him to sign a peace treaty." He takes a deep breath. "We've been at war for so long with the Pine Kingdom and lost so many men. My father may seem like a hard and difficult man, but he's only looking out for the best interests of his people. Every time we attack one another, too many lives are lost. Women lose their husbands. Children lose their fathers. It's been going on for so long that I don't even know the root cause. For me, it's personal. I want vengeance for the slaying of Leo. I don't want a war, only one man. Your father." The fury is evident in his eyes.

I can't blame him for wanting to fight the person that killed someone who meant so much to him. My father could have had his own reasons for killing him, though. I don't know. There are too many questions up in the air. All of which I wish I had answers to so I could make the best decisions for myself. I really wish my mother would have told me about this place when she was still alive.

Then his words really sink in. "He wants to trade

me?" I start to tremble.

Lucas' hand rests on my forearm. "I told him there has to be another way. That I won't let him place you in the hands of that monster." My inner voice points out that Lucas could be a monster, too. Oliver did say he's seen him kill. I need to go with my gut above everything else. It has never lead me astray, and right now, it's saying that Lucas is my best hope and that I can trust him.

"Alison, I promise to keep you safe. I will guard you with my life."

I scoff. "Oliver said something similar, that he would protect me."

His hand drops from my arm and he starts to pace the floor in front of me. "That horrible knight! You should forget you ever laid eyes on him. He's no good."

"Is it true that I was promised to him? That I'm his?"

He turns sharply to face me and takes two long steps, until his face is only inches from mine. "You are not his," he bites out. "And if I have my way, you never will be."

What does he mean, his way? My head is swimming with everything that has happened today, and I start to get dizzy. I reach out to steady myself, only there is nothing for me to grab. Lucas grips my arm and holds me up. He escorts me over to a chair at a table. I sit with my head in my hands and my eyes closed.

"You're clammy," he notes. "When was the last time you ate?"

I don't lift my head. "Yesterday."

"No wonder. Stay there. I'll prepare a meal for you." I don't have the strength to tell him no. I can eat the bar I have in my bag. My bag!

"Lucas, where is my backpack?" I ask nervously.

He points to the chair opposite of me. "I asked one of my men to bring it here while I went to retrieve you. I only trust them for now; not the other guards and not my father."

I release my breath as I see my bag there and open it up. The pewter box is in it along with clothes and other items. "Did he go through my things?"

"Yes. He said he wanted to make sure you weren't carrying anything that could harm us, but I have a feeling he was looking for something." If he knows where I'm from, then I wonder if my letter wasn't the first time he's heard about the mysterious skeleton key that rests in my pocket. I'm glad I had the forethought to keep it on me and not put it back in the box.

Resting my head back in my hands, my eyes flutter closed again. I must have drifted off, because the next thing I know, Lucas' hand is on my shoulder, and he's gently saying my name while he shakes me slightly.

I blink my eyes a few times and focus on his handsome features. He's sinfully sexy. I can't help all of the lustful thoughts running rampant in my sleep fogged mind. What I wouldn't give to feel his lips pressed to mine. Would they be soft? Would his hands be gentle when he touched me? I bite my lower lip.

"Alison?" His voice snaps me out of my daydream.

"Sorry, what?"

He gives me a lopsided smile. "Dinner is ready." Dinner. Is that at what part of the day we're at? I'm so disoriented I have no idea what time it is. It feels much later to me, but I notice the sun setting through the window.

Looking down, I see a brushed silver plate filled with noodles, stew, and a buttered roll. "You didn't have to go to so much trouble."

"Nonsense," he says. "I had the stew already made. It was only a matter of heating it up and cooking the noodles." My stomach lets out a loud grumble and I dive in. I didn't realize how hungry I am. Sure, I feel weak, but I thought it was due to all I had been through today.

He sits across from me and eats. We don't talk, however it's not uncomfortable. We look at each other every now and then, both of us smiling. I wonder what he's thinking. Here's this strange woman in his home, that he doesn't know, and is his enemy's daughter. Yet, I'm welcomed and he's fed me.

As I'm finishing up, my nerves start to act up. I'm alone with Lucas in his home. Am I to sleep here? If so, where? I look around the space and see a comfortable living area, the kitchen and stairs to an upper level. Maybe there's more than one bedroom. I wouldn't mind sharing a bed with him. Maybe we could do more than sleep. Damn, I need to get ahold of myself. I haven't been with anyone since my ex. I don't know if rushing into something with Lucas would be smart. Hell, I don't know if he even wants me that way.

I stand when he's finished and bring our dishes to the sink, much to his dismay. He insists I sit down, and he'll take care of everything, but I refuse. I tell him I'm feeling much better. I offer to wash the dishes and he stands beside me to dry.

"Do you want to go somewhere with me?" he asks shyly.

I look over to him and see his head is down, concentrating on making sure the plate he's holding doesn't have a drop of water left on it.

"Depends. It's not back into the dungeon, is it?"

His head snaps up and his eyes go wide. "What? No!"

I gently bump my shoulder into him. "I'm only kidding. I'd love to go somewhere with you." Now that I've eaten, I have some of my energy back.

He nods, nudges me back, and goes back to work drying.

CHAPTER SIX

Tali

Lucas puts the dishes away and hesitantly takes my hand in his. If I didn't know better, I'd think he really is shy. He's a completely different person when we're alone than he is in front of others, especially his father.

We walk outside, all the while he keeps a steady hold of my hand. I don't see anyone until we walk for a bit. There are four guards standing outside of a massive structure. I have to tip my head back to see the top of it. The men bow to Lucas, but don't speak. One opens the door for us and we step through.

There are huge bays on the inside. It almost reminds me of a massive barn for horses, only I doubt that's what is in here. They would have to be enormous steeds. A low rumble has the floor vibrating and I jump, pushing myself closer to Lucas.

He chuckles beside me. "Don't worry. Nothing in here will harm you. Come." He wraps his arm over my shoulders and we go further into the area. Every door on the stalls is a deep blue, deeper than the flowers in the field. About halfway through, we stop in front of a door that is much brighter than the others. It's the vibrant azure color I've seen throughout the castle. The name Talethla is painted across the front in a bright white. Then I feel the rumble again, but this time it's coming from behind the door in front of me. I try to back away, but Lucas isn't letting me.

"Alison, I want you to meet Tali. My dragon." That explains everything I've seen and heard. This is where the dragons are kept. How many are in here? I didn't bother counting the stalls. I've only seen the dragons in the sky and that was from a distance. The spaces in here are as big as houses. Some are larger than others.

Lucas unlatches the door and swings it wide. "Does that really hold them in there?" I ask.

"No. Some of the dragons prefer being alone, while most like to sleep with others. We tailor each area to the dragon. Tali likes being on her own, and the door being shut gives her the quiet she likes. The dragons are a large clan. They like to be together, some more than others," he chuckles.

"I've always pictured dragons living deep in a

cave or on a mountain top."

"They do. We have dragon familes that live throughout the lands, but these dragons..." He inclines his chin toward the huge stall. "...we hand raised them. They prefer to be with us, since we've been with them since birth. Tali, for instance, is only five years younger than me."

"Interesting."

My attention is drawn into the stall. It's dark and there's a rustle in the back. I can't see anything, but can feel a slight breeze on my cheeks. It comes in a burst. I assume it's Tali breathing.

I'm looking into the pitch-black darkness waiting for her to emerge. The first thing I see is her white face, horns pointing out from all angles. Her amethyst eyes are trained right on us, me more specifically. I try to move back, but Lucas isn't letting me. His arm is around my waist, holding me to him.

"Stay still," he whispers.

She inches closer, lifting her head to sniff he air. I've never been more afraid. Even the king throwing me in the dungeon didn't scare me as much as I am right now. Her strong legs come into view. Long claws tip each toe. Her wings are folded down by her side. Multiple shades of white and grey make up her scales. She's massive. Taller than the ranch houses back home, and now she's only feet from us. Her head lowers as she approaches. I want to run, flee, and get away from this powerful beast.

A few more steps and she's in my face, her large, horned nose in front of mine. She inhales, taking in my scent. When she lets her breath out, she blows my hair back. I still don't move. I'm frozen. Lucas is still as well. Is he afraid? I don't know what kind of relationship he has with his dragon.

Tali prods me with her nose, but her nudge pushes me backward. Luckily, Lucas is there to hold me up. She doesn't retreat. Her nose is pressed to me and I start to shake. The horns on her face scare me to no end. She has two on her chin that I'm waiting to see if they impale me. The one on her nose is at least pointed away from me.

She finally backs away, then turns slightly to Lucas. In one swift movement she's on her side with her foot pawing at him. She just barely misses nicking him with her claw. He releases me and walks forward to rub her neck. Her long tail swishes in contentment. She reminds me of a dog being petted by its master. Who knew a dragon could behave this way?

"Ali, come here," he beckons with one hand stretched out to me.

"Are you insane? I think I'll stay right here."

He chuckles. "She isn't going to harm you. If she was, she would have done it already."

Well, that's comforting. "Thanks for the warning. I could be dead right now."

"I wouldn't have let her hurt you. Now come

over here. The friendlier you become with her, the easier this will be."

"The easier what will be?" I ask. Although I'm not sure I really want to know.

"When we fly with her."

My mouth drops open. "When we what?"

"Fly. I want to show you my kingdom."

I start mumbling under my breath. "Crazy ass prince in this screwed up land wants to take me on the back of a dragon to fly through the clouds. Sure, why not? Not like I couldn't plummet to my death or anything."

"What?"

I plaster on a smile as not to show my nervousness. "Great idea."

Now I have to pet the dragon. I need to embrace the insanity of the moment and just do it. Taking hesitant steps, I walk to Tali and bend to rub her neck. Her head lifts, and she looks at me with those beautiful purple eyes. I wonder what she thinks of me.

She lies her head back down and I take that as an invitation to move forward. My hand cautiously touches her scales. They're warm and smooth. My fingers easily glide over her.

Lucas' leg brushes against mine. He whispers, "There. That wasn't so bad, was it?"

"Speak for yourself. At least I still have all of my limbs."

He laughs. "Are you ready to fly?" I know he directed the question to me, but Tali takes it as an invitation to get moving.

She jumps up, nearly knocking me back again. This time I'm able to steady myself on my own. Her tail starts swishing quickly and her eyes are big. She really wants to go.

"I'm sorry," Lucas says. "That's what I usually say to her to get her excited for some fun. I didn't think when I said it to you."

"Uh huh."

He pats Tali on the side and takes a few steps to me. He's close. If I leaned in I could press my lips to his. "Fly with me, Alison," he says in a deep timbre.

I'm lost in the color of his baby blue eyes. He leans in, and I close my eyes in anticipation, but a snort interrupts our moment. We break apart and look over to a very impatient dragon. Who would have thought? Tali is giving us attitude. It's probably for the best she disturbed us. I don't think kissing this handsome prince is the best idea. Of course, it would fit right in with this day.

Lucas turns to me with a mischievous grin. "I don't think she wants to wait. Let's go." He takes my hand in his, long fingers wrapping around mine.

He turns to leave the stall, pulling me with him.

Tali is on our heels. We exit the opposite way we came in. These doors are much larger to accommodate the dragons. Once outside, I notice the sky has darkened and the stars have made an appearance. The air is comfortable; the temperature has only dropped slightly. It makes me wonder if it's like this all of the time.

Tali walks to where the stone pathway elevates and seems to end atop the wall. I step forward and sure enough, it drops down into the water. No bridge on this side. If we fall, we're toast. Lucas pats her side and she sinks down to her belly. Her foreleg is bent to allow us to use it as a step to get on her.

He gestures for me to go ahead. One foot on her leg and I'm trying to figure out how to get on her back. "There's no saddle or anything?"

He shakes his head. "No. It makes her uncomfortable, and she can't maneuver as she needs to."

"How do you hang on?"

"Her scales. She has larger ones on her back that you can get a grip on."

"But, what if you fall?"

"I won't. We won't," he stresses. "I've flown with her so much that when we're in the air we fly as one. I'm able to predict her moves and know which way to lean."

"Kind of like riding on the back of a motorcycle."

His forehead scrunches. "A what?"

"A motorcycle. You don't have them here? What am I saying, of course you don't. Ignore me." I wave a hand in the air, hoping he'll drop it. We are about to fly. I can save the conversation about what a motorcycle is for another day.

Somehow, and I don't honestly know how, I manage to climb on Tali's back. With unbelievable grace, Lucas swings himself up behind me. He moves forward so his chest is pressed to my back. His legs hug the outside of mine. One strong arm wraps around my stomach and I lose my breath. He's so close. I can feel him everywhere. Oh, how I wish there were no clothes between us. Unconsciously, I lean my head back on his shoulder. He tenses for a second, then relaxes. There's a soft flutter on the skin at the base of my neck, causing goose bumps to break out over my body. His lips are feathering over my sensitive skin. I moan low in my throat.

"We should go," he says with his mouth below my ear.

"What if I want to stay like this?"

He chuckles. "I don't know how much patience Tali has. She's not known to sit still for long."

The dragon! I completely forgot we're sitting on the back of one. The haze in my lust-filled mind eases. "Right," I say, clearing my throat. "I'm ready."

"We'll see about that." He sits up tall behind me and grips me firmly. "Grab on to her, Ali." I'm afraid

I'm going to hurt her. My hands land on a section to hold onto and do I ever, because in the next breath, he yells, "Talethla, fly!"

Her giant wings spread slightly from her body and she takes a leap off the cliff. I try to scream, only nothing comes out. I'm going to die. Death by cliff diving dragon. Before we hit the water, her back arches, her wings stretch wide, and we start to curve toward the night sky. My stomach is in my throat, and I'm holding on for dear life.

We keep climbing, her wings flapping, and my eyes closed. I can't look. At any moment my body could be thrown off and plummet toward the ground. Yeah, I'm good with pretending I'm on a plane. At least then there is an enclosed cabin with seatbelts.

Her wings are situated just behind us. With each flap, we move with her. Eventually it feels like we are leveling out. My stomach starts to settle, but I still don't want to see how far up we are.

"Ali." My name from his lips floats across my skin. "Open your eyes."

"Nope. I'm good."

He laughs. "Would you trust me and open them? You don't know what you're missing."

"I believe I do. I'm missing the view of what I could land on if I fall."

"Okay, say you do fall. Tali is incredibly fast and

would be able to swoop down and catch you before you hit the ground."

I turn my head to look over my shoulder. "So, now you admit I could fall? Great. I knew it! This is when my life is going to end."

Thanks to the moon, I see his mouth lift into a smile. "Your life will not end today or any day that you're with me, my princess. That I promise you. I would sooner give up my own life than allow yours to be taken away."

I melt at his words. Damn, he's sweet. He leans forward and places a soft kiss at the corner of my mouth. My eyes flutter closed. "No, don't shut those beautiful eyes now that you have them open."

He takes his fingers and turns my head from his. "Holy shit!" I scream and launch myself onto Tali. My body is pressed to hers and I'm hanging on the best I can. Lucas' arm is still wrapped protectively around my waist. Tali turns to look at me like I'm some crazy human, then continues her flight. Every now and then Lucas tells her what direction to go in.

We dip to the right. I can see dim lights coming from buildings. I'm not quite sure what they are, since I don't know the layout of the land. The castle is easy to spot due to the many lights coming from it, its sheer size, and the way the lights reflect off the surrounding water.

"Why is the castle so bright, but not the other buildings outside of its walls?"

"We have electricity within the castle, however it hasn't been run to the connecting farms yet. We're still working through everything. It's new to us." It's amazing to me how this land is a mix of old and some more modern amenities like the electricity and hot water running throughout the castle. Such a paradox. Then I have an "aha moment" and wonder if that key was having some fun all of those years it laid in wait for me in the pewter box. Maybe it was busy bringing others to this realm through different doors. Interesting.

It's nice up here now that I've looked around. Not as scary as I thought. Maybe that's because I can't see much; I'm not sure. The wind causes my hair to whip around my face. Too bad I didn't bring a hair tie with me. Of course, who knew I was going to be flying on a dragon?

We fly for a while, I'm not sure how long. I see another large, lit up area in the distance, but we bank hard to the left before we can get close enough. I'm once again hugging the dragon, while my heart pounds in my chest.

"What's with the evasive maneuvering?" I yell.

"We reached the border of our land and sky. We have to stay within our boundaries."

"What was the place I saw lit up in the distance?"

"That was the Pine Kingdom." I stiffen. I'm not sure if it's from fear of my life, fear of the man who is my father being a ruthless killer, or fear that I may never meet him. I'm so conflicted. I don't know what to do. On one hand, he's my father. I'd like to hope that he would never hurt me. On the other, Lucas is adamant about me staying with him and that King Pine is a vicious man. If only I could meet him. Then there's Lucas. I want to stay safe with the man who is currently warming me in a way I thought had long gone dormant.

CHAPTER SEVEN

Question

Once Lucas feels me shiver in front of him, he decides to head back. We land safely on the side of the cliff where we jumped. I have to refrain from bending down and kissing the stone pathway under my feet. The ground never looked so good.

He takes my hand in his, and we walk back into the building with Tali close behind. As I watch her, she sniffs the air, and moves her head from side to side like she's scanning the area for potential threats. I hadn't noticed that before. She could be, but I don't know enough about her to know for sure.

Lucas swings the door to her area open wide. She doesn't go in right away. Instead, she stops in front of us and nudges me with her nose. I gently pat the side of her face as to not impale myself on any of her horns. I study her. Earlier I was too afraid to. Her amethyst eyes close as I continue to run my hand along her scales. Maybe she likes me after all.

Leaning down, I put my face near hers and rest my forehead on her briefly. She didn't let me die up in the air; that has to count for something. I need to show I trust her, even if it's not fully.

"She's warmed up to you," Lucas observes from beside me.

"I've warmed up to her, too."

He runs his hand next to mine, then ushers her inside. I stand by the door while he walks in. If I'm not mistaken, I hear him say, "I'm glad you like her." I smile, hoping that's what he said. I can't explain this attraction to him, but it's something that's existed since he first appeared in my dreams. Although, I couldn't see him well, I felt like I knew him. Never did I think he was real and was, in fact, having the same dreams as me.

He walks out and shuts the door before taking my hand. We stroll through the building hand-in-hand. He doesn't let go until we're tucked away back inside his home. Standing, facing one another, he looks into my eyes. I'm captivated by him. This evening has been much better than earlier. It almost makes up for me being thrown into a dungeon. Almost.

With a gentle hand, he reaches up to cup my cheek. His thumb skims along my skin. He leans forward and I think he's going to kiss me. I close my eyes anticipating his move, however his lips never touch me. I feel his forehead rest against mine. I open my eyes and see his are closed and his breath appears labored.

"Alison," he breathes. "How badly I want to kiss you."

"Then please do."

He shakes his head without losing contact with mine. "I don't want to push things with you. You're far too important for me to be rushing into something with you. I want to treat you right. I want to keep you on the pedestal you deserve to be put on. I want you to know just how much you've come to mean to me."

"Lucas—"

"Luke. Please call me Luke."

"Luke. You barely know me. I don't understand how you can feel so strongly."

He pulls back to look at me, his eyes searching mine. "And you feel nothing?"

"I didn't say that. It's just so quick. I don't know how to deal with it. You're supposed to get to know someone. Go on dates. Take your time, yet I want to skip all of that with you."

"You can go at whichever speed you wish. I'll be here regardless."

I start to swim in those blue eyes of his. "Kiss me."

"No. You deserve more. You deserve respect and admiration. I've been craving your touch for so long. Ever since you first appeared in my dreams, I've wished you were real. To have you standing before me, in my home, it's too much. I'm scared you're going to disappear, or I'm going to wake and this will all be another cruel dream that ends without you in my arms."

I warm all over at his words: so sweet and so real. I didn't know a man could speak his feelings this way. My ex-husband was a prick extraordinaire. He rarely told me how he felt; outside of saying he loved me every now and then. Even at that, it felt more forced than anything else. That was only the tip of the iceberg as to why things went downhill with him.

Here I am. Standing in a kingdom I knew nothing of a couple of days ago, in front of a prince who wants me. Me! Too bad I don't have any friends back at home who would swoon right along with me.

Then reality comes crashing down around me with a loud pounding at the door. Lucas, Luke, growls and his body goes rigid. "Stay behind me."

He opens the door, but fills the open space with his body, not letting the door open any wider. I remain hidden behind it.

"From the king, Your Highness," a masculine voice says. Luke nods and shuts the door.

He turns and I notice a piece of paper in his hands. His eyes shift back and forth as he reads it. "What does it say?" I ask.

He crumples the paper and throws it across the room. Turning away from me, he rakes a hand through his windblown hair. It makes me wonder, for a moment, what mine looks like. I dread trying to pull a comb through it.

He speaks while pacing. "My father wants us present for breakfast in the morning. Seems he wants to discuss the trade. King Pine is aware of your presence here." He faces me, his jaw hard with anger. "He wants you immediately sent to him. Oliver, too. My father hasn't responded yet. This is why he wants us at breakfast. To discuss things."

I immediately start to panic. "But...but I don't want to go. I want to stay here with you." I rush to him and fist the front of his shirt in my hands. I've gotten comfortable with Luke in the short time I've been with him. I truly believe he only wants to protect me. If I go to my father, I don't know what will happen. "Please. You can't let them trade me." Then there's Oliver. Will I be forced to marry him? To spend my life with a man I don't want to be with? I shiver thinking about it.

His hands grip my shoulders. "I won't let them take you from me. This I vow. Not now, not ever. Not when I've only just found you."

I bury my face in his shoulder. His arms wrap

around me, holding me close. I was foolish to think I was having a good night. My morning was great, because I met Luke. Then, bam! Shit hit the fan. I get freed from the dungeon and have a nice night with him and bam! Shit all over again.

"Maybe we can still keep you here. If my father had completely made up his mind he would have you taken away, and you'd be on your way to King Pine. There's something he wants. The question is what?"

"I have nothing to offer," I mumble into his shoulder. "All I've brought with me is my bag and the measly contents inside."

"You don't have any special abilities?"

I lift my head in surprise. "Seriously? Don't you think if I did, I would be a little more confident right now? Besides, it's not like I'm a witch or something and can cast spells."

He chuckles. "Witches aren't real. They're from stories we tell children."

"Uh huh. I didn't think dragons were real either, yet they are. I'm not ruling anything out."

"Come. Let's get you cleaned up and changed. You've had a difficult day and tomorrow could be worse." That's comforting. Worse. Tomorrow could be worse. Great. Can't wait.

He walks over to the table and retrieves my bag. Together we walk up the stairs to a large loft. There's a door off to one side that I assume is the bathroom.

On one wall is a large, four-poster, cherry wooden bed. There is black damask fabric hanging from the wooden top that's tied off on one side. The other is sealed in darkness. There is a matching nightstand on either side, with a lamp sitting atop each. On the opposite wall is a large wardrobe, but other than that the room is bare. Minimal.

He hands me my bag. "Here. Go clean up and warm yourself. Your skin is still cold from our flight. The bathroom is through there." He points in the direction of the other door in the room. "The water will take a moment to heat, but it will warm up nicely. Take as long as you need."

I nod, then remember I don't have any pajamas. "I didn't bring anything to sleep in," I admit shyly.

"That's okay," he says with a smile. Walking over to the wardrobe, he opens it, and pulls out a large, short-sleeved, navy shirt. "This should do well." He hands it to me and I immediately note how buttery soft the fabric is.

"Thank you."

I turn and walk to the bathroom. Gently closing the door behind me, I rest my back against it and take a few deep breaths. I'm worried about what's going to happen tomorrow. I could be shipped off to my father and never see Luke again, never see my home again.

Then again, I do have the key in my pocket. I could sneak out in the middle of the night and try to find the cottage. Although, there are guards along the wall surrounding the castle. I wouldn't be able to leave. If I'm honest with myself, do I really want to?

Tears sting my eyes, but I refuse to let them fall. I will be strong. Whatever happens I will stand and fight for what I want. King or not, I'm a princess here and that has to count for something.

Taking a few more breaths, I look around the bathroom. There's a simple porcelain sink on my left that sits on top of a dark wooden cabinet. There's a tub with a showerhead. I'm a little surprised to see the shower. I thought there would only be a tub, but then again, what do I know of a prince's bathroom? I would have thought he'd be with his family in the main part of the castle.

I undress quickly while the water heats and step under the warm spray. It doesn't take long to clean and wash my hair with what he has along the shower wall. Stepping out of the tub, I dry off, and slip into the soft shirt Luke gave me. I bring the fabric to my nose and inhale. It has a woodsy smell, just as his home did when I first entered it. Nothing like the awful smell of the dungeon I was in.

Finding a comb below the sink, I spend far too long trying to get the knots from my hair. Flying did a number on it. Using the towel one more time, I scrunch my hair, and drape the towel over the tub to dry.

I locate a toothbrush under the sink that appears

new. Hooray for the small things! I didn't even think to pack one. Next time I travel to a far off land, I'll remember to pack the essentials.

Rooting through my bag, I find and throw on a pair of underwear, but decide to forgo the bra. I may be sleeping in a prince's home, but I'm not going to spend the night with an uncomfortable underwire jabbing me in the boob while I sleep.

I grip the handle of the door, but hesitate. Luke is out there waiting for me. What will happen now? Where will I sleep? Could he possibly want to share a bed? He mentioned before about wanting me in his arms. The thought of sleeping beside him causes my stomach to flutter. I shouldn't be nervous. I've slept with other men before. No, they weren't princes, however I didn't know I was a princess either. I can do this. I'm a woman who craves a man; it's that simple or that complicated.

I exit the bathroom and find Luke sitting on the side of the bed with his head in his hands. Upon hearing the door open, he lifts his head and lets his eyes roam over my body. The shirt is long enough to cover my ass, but just barely. A slow blush creeps over my face while he takes his time raking me from head to toe with his gaze.

He stands slowly and makes his way toward me. I can't move. I'm frozen in place by the intense look on his face, like he wants to devour me. He stops before me and leans in to brush a kiss across my lips. He's gone before I can savor the contact. I turn in time to watch the bathroom door close gently.

Letting out a breath, I place my bag on the bed and remember that I left the skeleton key in my jeans, which I balled up and threw inside before I took a shower. I remove the key and take out the pewter box. I'm about to place it back inside when a little voice in my head tells me not to. Instead, I remember there's a small hidden compartment on the inside of the backpack. It's used to hide money when you travel. Reaching around within, I locate the small pocket and gently slip the key inside. Hopefully, it will remain safe there.

I move my bag to the floor near Luke's wardrobe and look around, not sure what to do with myself. I'd love to slip into bed, but it's not mine, and I don't know where I'll be sleeping. Finally deciding, I sit down on the edge of the bed and wait for Luke to finish in the shower.

Running my fingers through my hair out of nervousness, I remember I stashed hair ties in all of my bags at one point and know there are some in the backpack. At least there's that.

The bathroom door opens and Luke emerges. Holy mother of all that is good. He looks sexy as hell. Cotton pajama shorts rest low on his hips showing off the outline of an impressive dick. His chest is bare. His skin lightly tanned, and there's only a dusting of dark hair on his chest and abdomen. Each muscle on him is well defined, but his abs show off just how fit he is. Each small ridge dips and flows into the next one, all the way down to a delicious V on his hips. His biceps are large and flex nicely when he combs back his hair with his hand.

His eyes meet mine and I know he caught me checking him out. There's no way I could help it when he came out here looking like he did. This girl isn't dead yet and is very unattached. I appreciate a fine male body when I see one. Especially when that body is of the prince I've been dreaming of.

He walks toward me like a wild cat after prey. His steps are graceful, yet precise. If he didn't know the effect he has on me, he does now, because I actually start fanning myself with my hand. When I realize what I'm doing I quickly stop. Smooth move on my part. Real smooth.

Stopping only a foot in front of me, Luke peers down. My mouth goes dry and I instinctively lick my lips. His eyes flash to them, watching the movement my tongue makes.

His voice is low and rough. "Move over."

I blink a couple of times and try to register what he said. Move over? Oh, right. I'm on the bed. I stand on shaky legs to get out of his way. His hand grips my wrist and he brings me back down to the bed.

"That's not what I meant. I wanted you to slide over. Not leave the bed all together."

He pulls the blankets back and insists, "Get in." I look at him, but don't say anything. Is he offering to sleep in bed with me? Or is he giving me the bed? I'm confused about what's going on.

"Alison, I want you to sleep in the bed. I can take the couch downstairs."

"The couch?" I swear it's like I've never been with a man before and am a newbie. I slide into bed.

His lips quirk up on one side. "We need to sleep. I can sleep on the couch downstairs or climb into bed with you. It's up to you. I only want you to be comfortable."

Now I understand him. He just wants to sleep. My stupid lust-filled brain can't even carry on a simple conversation. "I'd like you to sleep with me. In the bed!" I add quickly. "I mean you and I can share the bed." I bury my head in my hands as embarrassment floods me. Too bad I can't hide under the blankets.

The bed dips and strong arms and a bare chest envelope me. This is not helping in the least. He chuckles. "Ali, lie back. We're only sleeping. Nothing more."

Lifting my head, I look at him with what I'm sure is a face as red as a cherry and nod. I can't speak. Who knows what would come out of my mouth if I did.

I lie back and look up at the black damask. Luke shuts the light off, pulls the fabric closed, and settles next to me. I turn my head and see he's facing me. "Hi," he says softly.

"Hi."

"Roll away from me. I want to hold you."

I do as he says. His arm reaches over me and pulls me flush against him, my back to his chest. He's warm and smells like the soap in the shower. I wiggle in as close as possible. He starts to harden behind me, causing me to freeze. I would love nothing more to reach around and hold onto him, to explore every inch, but if that's what he wants he wouldn't have asked me to move.

"Relax, Ali. Sleep."

I find a comfortable spot for my head on the pillow and eventually drift off with his warm breath on my neck, and his body encasing me in security and heat.

CHAPTER EIGHT

Ultimatum

Morning comes far too fast. I'm not sure of time anymore, since I don't have a watch and haven't seen a clock, which now that I think about it is a little odd. I probably just missed one. I know it isn't the sun that wakes me since the damask is still closed. No, it's the man behind me, nuzzling into my neck with his soft lips and coarse facial hair. And what a great way to wake up it is.

Luke's voice is still thick with sleep. "Good morning, my princess."

There's something that warms in me every time he calls me his princess. His. But am I his? Or am I Oliver's? No, I'm no one's, even if I love hearing him say that. I'm my own person.

"Morning," I reply.

"I wish we could stay in bed all day, but knowing my father, one of his men will soon be here banging on my door to ensure we arrive on time." Goodbye momentary happiness, hello complete uncertainty and fear.

Groaning, I sit up and run my fingers through my hair. Hopefully it doesn't look as frizzy as it feels. The bed moves as Luke gets up. He opens the dark fabric and light streams in. I have to squint to deal with the sudden change.

"I'm sorry," he chuckles. "I should have warned you."

"What time is it?"

"Time to get up." I turn to look at him and notice he's as sexy fresh out of bed as he is when he lies down. How is that even possible? His hair is perfectly messed.

I turn away before I start drooling. "Don't you have a clock around here?"

"A clock?"

"It's a way to tell time."

"We have no need for one. My body knows when it's time to rise. The sun guides us; we live by our bodies and what they need."

"That's interesting," I mumble.

He walks to my side of the bed and opens the damask. The smile on his face is infectious. I return it with one of my own. "You'll get used to it, Ali."

"I don't know. That's if I stay." The words slip out before I have a chance to think about them. Now we're going to have an entire other conversation I don't want to have.

His brows furrow. "Why wouldn't you stay?"

I let out a breath. "Luke, this world is yours, not mine. Your father is talking about trading me to my father, like I'm nothing more than a tool to get what he wants, not a person. I don't even know if I want to meet my father, let alone live in his kingdom. And what about Oliver? I'm just supposed to marry him if I'm made to live there?" I shake my head. "I don't want to be forced into anything." I'm trying to skirt the issue and not bring up the door or the key, although I have a feeling I'll need to.

His jaw tenses and his tone is firm. "You will not have to marry that...that poor excuse for a knight! You'll stay here, in the Azure Kingdom, with me. I won't let them take you away."

"What if you don't have a choice? Your father is king, which means what he says goes. I should go back home. That would be best for everyone."

"That would not be what's best. I don't want you to leave, Ali. I just found you."

I place my hand on his arm. "Luke, this is your home, not mine. I don't want you to have to fight with your father for me. We've only just met."

"You're worth it."

"I'm not. I'm just an ordinary person who's trying to find her way in life."

"And your way led you here. Everything happens for a reason, Alison. Our dreams, finding each other, we were meant to meet. Now it's up to us to continue on that path."

"We can always alter the path, Luke. It's what makes our lives our own."

He nods. "That's true, but in the end we'll end up where we were always meant to be."

No matter what I say at this point, it won't do me any good. I know he means well, and he truly believes we were brought together for a reason. I've never put much faith in fate, or anything, for that matter. I'm going to have to take each moment as it comes. Deal with the blows today that I'm sure will come, one at a time.

I stand and try to walk past Luke to go to the bathroom. I only make it one step before his arm shoots out to block me across my waist. He looks to me, piercing me with his blue eyes.

"When you stepped into my path in the field of azure flowers, flowers of my kingdom, everything changed. The sky seemed bluer, the stars became brighter. True, when I first found out who your father is, it set me on the defensive, but once I read the letter, it all made sense. I feel like I have a greater purpose now. Yes, my job is to guard my people and land, but the high I got fighting is nothing compared to how I feel when I'm with you. When your hand touches mine, or you smile, it feels right. You're my dream come true. I won't let you go when I've been wanting you for so long."

"Luke, I —"

Pulling me in front of him, he cuts of my words with his lips. This isn't the quick brush of lips we had before. No, this kiss is heated, and I feel it down to the tips of my toes. His arms reach around me to pull me flush against his strong chest. All of the thoughts as to why I should leave this place, flee my mind. Luke is all that matters in this moment.

My body relaxes in his hold, molding to him. His tongue caresses my lips, urging me to invite him in. I know once I taste him I'll be addicted. The notion scares me and excites me at the same time. The more I let him in, the harder it will be to leave if I choose or am forced to.

My heart overrules my head. My lips part, allowing him access. He wastes no time in his exploration of me. Tears threaten to escape my closed eyes. He's perfect: his taste, his passion about wanting me, his vow to protect me. I don't know what I did to deserve this from someone I only met yesterday. I'm afraid he will be ripped away from me in a matter of hours. This intense need and pull to him could be gone. I don't know what the king wants with me, but I doubt it will be good.

We stand kissing for a minute more before his mouth breaks away. I can feel how much he wants me. His hardness is pressing against my lower stomach, only making me wild in my desire for him. He holds me close, his breath tickling my neck.

"Nothing will keep us apart. Not my father, not King Pine, and especially not Sage. There is always a way, Ali. We only have to find it."

I nod, however don't speak. I will end up full on crying if I do. So much is up in the air. Most importantly, my future.

❖

I'm dressed in the spare clothes I brought, a light blue t-shirt and a pair of jeans, when we exit Luke's home and walk through the morning bustle of people to have breakfast with the king. We've caught the eyes of the locals again. I'm sure my presence here made for good gossip for all of them over dinner last night, especially since I'm holding hands with one of their princes.

Luke is dressed in matching navy cotton pants and t-shirt. The way the shirt forms to him like a second skin had my breath faltering before we left. I couldn't stop staring, which is oh so becoming. All I needed was to let my tongue hang out of my mouth. That would have solidified things with him. I mean, who could resist that?

I also watched as he strapped knives to each leg, while I placed my bag on my back. He contemplated strapping his swords on his, but thought he might be perceived as more of a threat if he did. He was sure to stress that he wanted to be able to protect me if the need arose. While he said his father is a good man, he will put the well-being of his people above mine. I honestly wouldn't expect him to side with me.

I did ask Luke about how his father knew about where I was from. He was as confused as I was and said he did ask, but his questions were left unanswered.

We reach the same room I first met the king in, but this time it's decked out for a feast and smells of delicious food. Meats, spices, pastries, it's overwhelming and leaves my mouth watering. As nervous as I am about what will happen, I know I need food to maintain my strength. I've never been one of those people who gets nervous and doesn't eat. Quite the opposite. Nerves and food go hand-in-hand for me.

The king is standing as we enter. The only other people in the room are his guards. I have no idea if I'm supposed to bow or curtsey, and I honestly don't care. This man locked me up and released me, only to say he wants to trade me. I'm not a pawn nor will I be handled as one. I will not bow to him or anyone else in this realm.

"Lucas, Alison, nice of you to join us," he says,

almost overly sweetly with a nod of his head. I respond in kind with a nod. That's all he's getting from me and because he did the same. "Let's sit. We have plenty to discuss."

Luke pulls out a chair for me. He once again puts himself between the king and me. I don't know the proper etiquette for eating with royalty, so I wait for Luke to eat before taking a bite. The food is as good as it smells. I could seriously get used to eating like this. I also would need to work out like crazy, because I can imagine the amount of weight I'd gain.

We eat in silence for a few minutes when the king speaks. He looks to his guards and commands, "Leave us." They bow and exit the room, closing the door behind them.

"I know you didn't invite us here simply for food. Shall we get started?" Luke asks. I pick up an edge of steel in his voice.

"You were always confrontational, my son. It's what makes you an excellent leader of my guard." Luke nods in confirmation. King Azure turns to me. "Alison, we both have something the other wants. If you give me what I ask for, then I'll grant your freedom. You may live in my kingdom and have our protection from any threat toward you, including your father. You will become one of us. No one will force you to leave, but if one day you choose to meet your father, we will send the Elite by your side to ensure no harm befalls you."

My eyes narrow. He needs something I have. I have nothing, but this gives me leverage to get my way. I have a bargaining chip at this table. "And what if I don't want to give you what you seek?" Luke's head snaps in my direction. His eyes are wide, like I just said something completely foolish. Maybe I did. Or maybe I just started playing the game.

"You either accept my rules or I will have you escorted, with your intended husband, to the border of my land in exchange for my men that are being held by King Pine. I also will have him sign my peace treaty in exchange for you and Sage."

"Okay, let me get this straight. You're giving me an ultimatum? Either I give you whatever it is you want, or you'll trade me to get something else you're in need of. You win, no matter which I choose."

He smiles, but it's not kind. He knows the ball is in his court. I was foolish to think I had a leg to stand on. Either way, I lose. Wait. What do I lose if I stay here? "What do you want from me in exchange for my freedom?"

He leans forward, putting both elbows on the table and steeples his fingers. "You have a key that I would like." The key. Of course! No wonder he went rifling through my bag. My mother warned me about keeping the key safe. She didn't want it to fall into the wrong hands.

"Why do you want it?"

"That's for me to know."

"Oh, but I don't think it is. You know as well as I do from my mother's letter, that the key has a mind of its own. I do have it, for now, and if you want this key from me, I want to know why."

His voice hardens. "Don't test me. You may be a princess, but I am under no obligation to keep you well. King Pine asked for you alive. That's it. He didn't say you couldn't be locked up and starved." I gasp. Here is the hard side of the king again.

Luke hasn't said a word up until this point. Only watched our conversation like a spectator at a tennis match, his head going back and forth. His tone is placating. I'm not sure what he's up to. "Father, may I have a word with Alison alone? I promise not to leave the premises. Grant us a few moments in another room. Your men can stand guard, but I want privacy."

"As you wish, but don't push me, Lucas. A few moments and nothing more."

Luke nods and stands. He holds out his hand for mine and helps me from my seat. We leave the room with two guards on our heels and step into an adjoining room. Luke shuts the door and turns to me.

"What's going on, Ali? Why don't you give him the key?"

I turn from him and start to pace the room. At this point, I'm screwed either way. If I don't give him the key then I'm going to be shipped off with Oliver to the other kingdom where I'll be forced into marrying a man I don't know and living a life I didn't choose. He knows I have the key, but he doesn't know where it is. I really should have hidden it better.

I'm lost in my own thoughts when I hear Luke yell my name. "Alison!" I stop and look at him. His posture is tense. I instinctively take a step back. I get another glimpse of the tough side of him now. When he sees me step away from him, he visibly relaxes.

"I'm sorry," he says. "I didn't mean to snap at you, but we have limited time. I need you to talk to me. I need you to tell me about this key. You have something my father wants. We need to be able to use that to our advantage."

"Luke, I'm putting my trust in you, and you need to do the same with me."

"Of course. I told you I'd protect you."

"I know you did, but this goes beyond that. My mother, she died of cancer a year ago." I swallow the emotion clogging my throat, as it always does when I speak of her.

"My mother died too. I was only a child, though."

"I'm sorry you didn't have her growing up."

He shrugs. "I don't really remember her. My siblings do, however."

I clear my throat and try to get back on topic, or we'll be here all day and the king said we had only moments alone. "Do you remember the letter my mom left me?" He nods. "In it she mentioned the key has a mind of its own. It's unpredictable. But she did say that if I still have the key when I cross over to your realm that I can use it to get back. There is no guarantee that I can ever return here. Once I go back home it could disappear forever. If I give the key to your father, not only would I never be able to leave, but he could bring his entire army through the door back to my world. He could release a small dragon. We don't have them there! They are something only in books or movies."

"What's a movie?"

I shake my head. "Later. My point is that he could use it for malicious intent, and I would never be able to go back home."

"I see your point about not knowing what he wants it for. We don't know for sure what he will do with it. I also told you that this is your home now. You don't have to go back."

"We just met, Luke," I stress, exasperated. "Would you give up your whole world, everything you know, for me?"

With a completely serious look on his face, he answers firmly. "Yes."

"How can you be so sure about me? About us?"

He closes the distance between us and cups my cheeks in his hands. Looking down into my eyes, he reiterates what he told me before. "You have come here for a reason and I found you. We haven't only just met. We've known each other. No, we didn't talk in our dreams, but we did establish a connection. One that I can't deny nor can you, because if you could, you would have tried to leave and return home. You haven't, though. Instead, you slept in my arms."

"My heart tells me to stay and be with you, but my head is saying to be logical, to think this through." He'd give up everything for me. Could I ask him to, though? What if I could bring him home with me? He's only ever known this land and he's proud of it. Proud of who his family is and the fact he's a fighter. He wouldn't fit in back home. That much I know for sure. He doesn't belong there. Do I belong here? Maybe, maybe not.

"You don't have much time to do that. My father expects an answer when we walk back in, or you will be leaving here. You'll be leaving me. I will fight for you, but I can't say what will happen. If I'm hurt or killed, I won't be able to protect you. With me gone, I fear what would happen. You have a decision to make, my princess. Will you stay here, with me? Will you follow your heart? Or will you take your key and flee back to the cottage? Will you leave me behind?"

CHAPTER NINE

Choices

Where the hell is a crystal ball when you need one? How am I supposed to make this decision? My problem is that I know what I want to do. I'm afraid I'll regret the decision; that it will be the wrong one, and I won't be able to go back, because even if I go home, I might not be able to come here ever again. If I give the key to King Azure, who knows if I'll ever see it again. There is the slimmest of chances that it could return to me, but what if it decides to stay with him or finds someone else? Stupid key. I wish I had time to weigh everything.

A loud knocking makes me jump, followed by a gruff voice, "Your Highness. The king is requesting your presence along with Princess Pine."

"That is not my name!" I screech.

Luke chuckles. He walks to the door and holds it open for me. "We must go. You have until we walk next door to decide." No pressure. None at all.

We walk back into the room where the scent of breakfast engulfs me once again. Taking our seats, I look at my plate and try to steady my breathing. In the time it took us to walk from one room to the next, I've become extremely nervous. If I think about it, I should be one big ball of raw nerves by this point.

Every day we're faced with choices in our lives. Do we go this way or that? Drive down one street or the other? Do we take a leap and jump into the unknown? Or do we stay on the steady and safe course? Every day you make choices that have the ability to alter your life. You have the choice to trust your head or follow your heart. They don't always align, but when they do, you need to follow them, because it's rare.

"Do you have an answer for me, Princess?" the king asks.

I lift my head to look at him. Luke is watching me intently, however showing no emotion. "I do have an answer, but it comes with a question that must be answered first and a few conditions. If you don't agree to this, then we're only left with one option." I'm silently hoping he agrees, because everything is depending on this. I know how badly he wants the key and the peace treaty. He can't have both, though. At least not right now.

"What's the question?"

"No bullshit. No games. I want a straight answer." The king's mouth lifts ever so slightly into a smile, which surprises me. "Why do you want the key?"

His mouth settles back into his version of showing no emotion. I'm getting zero read off of it. "I want it to find my love."

"Your love?" I inquire.

"Yes, the only woman I've ever loved. She's in your world. Every moment without her my soul aches." His fist tightens and he brings it to his chest to punctuate what he's saying.

Luke's head whips around to face his father. "What? What about Mom? I know she's gone, but did you love her? Doesn't her memory garner more respect than this? I can't believe you had someone else."

King Azure lets out a long breath. "Lucas, I would never disrespect your mother. The truth is, she didn't die. She fled our realm, and she did it with Eliza Wescot." The room starts to spin, and I place my hands onto the arms of my chair to steady myself.

"She's...she's alive? Mother's alive?" Luke questions, barely above a whisper.

"Yes, my son, she is. At least as far as I know. Alison's mother and yours were very close friends, even though King Pine and myself forbade it. They found ways to stay in touch with one another and spend time together. They trusted each other. We knew, of course we knew, but they were our wives. How do you say no to the person you love most in the universe? Especially when you see how happy having a friend who understands all they are going through, makes them."

My mind reels with the information. It also starts to put things together. I remember my mom having a best friend, someone who she only saw once a year, but who she spoke of fondly. "Rya," I whisper.

"What?" It's Luke who asks. The surprise evident in his voice.

"My mom had a friend who she saw only every once in while, but they spoke often. Her name was Rya."

"That's my mother's name."

"Alison, is Rya alive?" the king asks.

"Yes." I nod. "Last I knew, anyway. I saw her at my mom's funeral a year ago. We didn't speak much during the service. She seemed as upset as I was. She came to town for it, but I don't know from where. My mom never told me where she lived."

The king's eyes start to well with tears, but he's able to hold them back. I look to Luke and he doesn't appear to be holding it together much better. He believed his mother was dead, only to find out that she's alive. I can't imagine what that must feel like: shock, relief, anger at his father.

He stands abruptly, forcing the chair to fall back onto the floor. He points to his father, "You lied to me! You lied to all of us! We believed our mother was dead. Why? Why would you do that? We're your children!"

The king scrubs a hand over his face. "I didn't have a choice." In this moment he isn't a king; he's a heartbroken man who lost his wife. No, she might not be dead, but she hasn't been with him in many years. "King Pine and I were at war. Eliza was pregnant and scared. Rya didn't like the war that was going on. When Eliza said she was leaving, Rya went with her. I tried to stop her, but your mother was very headstrong. King or not, she never listened to me. The key you have, Alison, it could bring me to my wife who I haven't seen in almost twenty-four years."

"Wait," Luke interrupts. "I don't understand why she would leave her four children here." He leans down with his hands braced on the table.

"The war wasn't her only reason for leaving. She was pregnant. Your mother was carrying twins." Luke feels around for his chair, only to discover it's still lying on the floor. He rights it and takes a seat.

"Twins?"

The King nods. "She started bleeding and our healer didn't know what was happening. Our medicine isn't as advanced as it is in Alison's world. Eliza stressed that the doctors in Colorado could help her. She even drew a map for me of where her home was and where the hospital was in relation to it. That's why I asked Alison about the Rocky Mountains. They were near where Eliza lived. But you see, I didn't have the skeleton key, so I couldn't go there. I also couldn't leave you and your siblings here without both parents. You were all so young. The war ended and life went on without her. I didn't want to give all of you hope she'd come back, when after some time she didn't. So I told you she passed away.

My mom was born in the U.S. I know that for a fact having seen her birth certificate. She must have gotten the key at some point, crossed into this realm, and stayed here for years. She got married and became queen. Had Reid and gotten pregnant with me. There's so much about her life I'll never know.

"I've waited every day for her to return. Wished, hoped, and visited the cottage often. Why do you think that old building still stands on the outskirts of the woods? I'm waiting for her to come back. It's the only way she can come here. What I never understood is why she hasn't. Now I know Eliza kept the key, but I'm sure she would have given it to Rya to return. It doesn't make any sense."

Luke turns to me. "Do you recall my mother having children?"

I shake my head. "My mom never offered much information about Rya. What I was told was minimal, at best. Like there was a great secret I couldn't be told and now I know why. She never told me about this realm until she was gone."

"We don't know if the twins survived," Luke mutters.

"Could my father have killed Leo, because Rya and my mom left? As revenge in some messed up way?"

Luke's face drops, but then changes into anger. "I don't care his reasoning. The fact remains that he did it knowing full well what he meant to me." I can't help but think that's part of the reason he did it. I could be way off base and he's just that ruthless. I don't know if I'll ever know for sure.

I can't believe all that's being said. My mom was best friends with Luke's mom. They were both pregnant and they fled together.

"This is the most messed up fairy tale ever," I observe.

The king scoffs. "Princess, a fairy tale would imply there is a happily ever after. I have yet to see that for anyone."

"But there's still time," I stress. "You can go through the portal and find her. You can use the key to get her back."

"That's what I'd like to do. If she'd even want to come back to me after all of these years. There must be a reason she never returned. I hope she still loves me."

"Maybe the key wouldn't stay with her. My mom said it would disappear and reappear. For all we know Rya did try to take it, but it wouldn't stay with her long enough to use." I know it's only a theory. It's better than nothing, though.

I stand and reach for my backpack, which is resting on the chair beside me. I unzip it and notice all of my belongings in disarray. Turning to the king, I accuse, "You went through my things again!"

"No, I didn't. One of my men did."

"Same thing!"

I go back to my bag to find the key. In all reality, I should have known he'd look through my things. If I were in his position, and was left alone in a room with something I had been in need of for years to find the love of my life, I probably would have ripped it to shreds.

I find the heavy key in its hidden compartment and hold it tight in my hand. My choice is made. This is bigger than me. There is an entire family who has missed their mother and wife. I can't be the one to keep her from them.

King Azure has waited too many years; I can't make him wait any longer. Sure I could go back and find her, but she barely knows me. What if once I'm through, the key disappears? Then he's still stuck without his wife. There is no guarantee. He has a better chance at convincing his wife to return. For all I know, she could have thought he would move on without her. Who knows what she's thinking? He needs to find her, however. That is, if the key wants him to use it.

I walk to the king. He rises and looks into my eyes. What I see is a man who has been lost for so long without the other half of his soul. My chest aches for him. I hold out my hand, palm up, exposing the key. He inhales a ragged breath. When he reaches for it I close my hand fast. I have to remember the conditions.

"You need to agree to my conditions before I hand this key to you." He nods. "First, you must agree not to bring any weapons with you. Second, no one will go through with you. You must go on this mission alone. Third, you cannot tell anyone in my land about where you're from or how you got there. You can say you're a friend of the family or something if you're asked. And you mustn't tell anyone here where you've been if you do come back. You'll have to make up a story about your wife and where she's been. My world must remain hidden, as must yours, from the people on the other side."

"I agree," he states.

"I will help you find something suitable to wear, so that you'll fit in. I'll tell you where I have cash and credit cards kept in my home. I'll tell you everything that I can to help you. In fact, in my phone on my nightstand is Rya's number. You'll have to use it to contact her. In return, I want what you promised me. I want immunity. You will not force me to go to my father or Oliver. I will become a citizen of the Azure Kingdom. You will also provide me with all of the same benefits that your children have. Money, a home, everything."

"Of course. Luke will see to it all, won't you, Son?"

"What?" he asks, obviously not paying attention. "I'm sorry. I'm still trying to process everything."

"Alison. She will be your responsibility to protect and ensure she has everything she needs. She will be one of us and treated as royalty amongst our people."

He tenses and rises to meet us. "Of course. I wouldn't have let you trade her, even if that were her choice."

The king smiles warmly. "I already knew that."

"You did?" Luke questions.

"Of course. I saw the way you looked at her when you first brought her in. I knew she was special to you."

"You still played her."

"Yes, and I'm not sorry for it either. I need to find my Rya. I would have done whatever it took to get that key."

I interrupt. "Oddly, I'm not even angry about that." I reach for the king's hand and place the key in it. Surprisingly, it remains solid in his palm. I didn't know what it would do. "Protect this with your life."

"On my honor," he pledges, with the key pressed to his heart, then he turns to Luke. "We have a lot to discuss. I need to fill your brothers and sister in. We need Ryland to take over the throne once I'm gone. We'll have to devise a plan as to what to tell our people." Luke nods.

"No one outside of your immediate family can know the truth," I stress. Hopefully the guards outside can't hear our conversation.

"I agree," the king replies. "The less who know, the better."

CHAPTER TEN

Family

We leave the king's chambers after I pick out some simple clothing for him that should allow him to blend in. Luckily, his hair is done nicely, making him look refined.

Luke and I walk back to his home. We're to return at sunset for dinner when he will tell Luke's brothers and sister the plan. While apart, I will be writing down everything I can think of for the king. Instructions on where to go, how to use my phone, and a host of other things. I'm hoping that once he gets ahold of Rya, she will come to him. He won't know how to use a car and there are no cabs in my small town. I won't be there to assist him, but I can give him the most information possible. He will have to remain in my home and wait for her.

Once inside, Luke hands me paper and a pencil. I sit at the table and begin to quickly write. He strides to the couch and throws himself onto it. His arm bends to rest over his eyes. The sight of him makes my chest pinch. He's been through so much this morning. I try to write faster, so I can spend some time with him before we have to go back for our meeting with his family.

When I finally think I have everything covered and my hand is completely cramped up, I fold the paper and leave it on the dining table. Standing, I walk to the couch where Luke hasn't moved since he laid down. I sit on the edge facing him, and place my hand on the arm he has lying by his side. The one covering his face lifts and he peers up at me. In his eyes I see sorrow, hurt, and hope. Most of his life he thought his mother was dead, and not only is she alive, but he could have more siblings. There is also the possibility that she won't come back, or his dad for that matter. My heart breaks for him.

He reaches up, gently grips my arms, and pulls me down until I'm resting my head in the crook of his neck. I nuzzle it with my nose and relax in his arms. He's holding me tightly and I let him. He's not the only one who could use comfort at the moment. At least we have each other.

His heart is beating a steady rhythm beneath my palm. His voice is rough with emotion when he says, "Thank you."

I lift my head to look into his eyes. They are full

of unshed tears. "For what?"

"For sacrificing the ability to go back to your home, so my father can go in search of my mother. I know what you're giving up for us."

I gently caress the rough stubble on his cheek. "If he can find her and bring her back, my sacrifice will be worth it. Really, I don't have anything to go back to."

He cocks his head to the side. "What do you mean?"

I shrug one shoulder. "My mom was the only family I had there, and once she passed away I was alone. I had no real friends. I was living each day with no excitement, no real purpose other than fulfilling her wishes. At least here I have a father, albeit one that I don't know, nor am I sure if I want to. But if I'm here, then the opportunity is there for me to seek him out."

He brushes a stray piece of hair away from my face. "And here I thought that maybe you were staying here for me."

"You may have been a factor."

"May?"

I roll eyes. "Okay, so you were a factor."

"I knew it," he gloats.

"No one likes a bragger."

He laughs, takes my face in his hands, and lifts

his lips to mine. It's not the heated kiss of this morning. This one is more languid. Our tongues meet and sweep over one another. It's sweet.

I pull away before it can become more. "So," I say with my face tucked back into his neck, while my finger makes small circles on his chest. "Is there an unoccupied home nearby that I can move into? Seems I'm currently without one."

"You're joking."

"No, not at all. I need somewhere to live."

"You honestly believe that I'm going to let you sleep somewhere other than in my arms after I've spent the night with you, and know what pure bliss it is? That was the best sleep I've had in years. No, my princess, you'll be staying with me."

"Luke, we can't live together. That's really rushing it."

"Are we going to discuss this again?"

"Apparently so. I don't know what it's like here, but where I'm from you don't move in with someone after only knowing them a day. Okay, maybe a few people do, but it took me a year before I moved in with my ex-husband."

He sits up quickly, taking me with him. "You're married?"

I look at him and straddle his hips to get comfortable on his lap. "No, I'm not married. I said ex-husband. Emphasis on the ex part."

"Did he die?"

"No, but I could have killed him for cheating on me."

"What?" he shouts. "How could he have done that? How could anyone do that to you?"

"I asked myself that very question when I caught him in bed with another woman, but in the end it was for the best."

"We don't part once we're married here. When we say our vows, it's for life," he states firmly.

"We do, too, but sometimes it doesn't work out as planned."

His hands grip my hips and he pulls me flush against him. "Our worlds are different, but it matters not. I have you here with me. I'm never letting go. You can argue about how quick it is, and fight me along the way, but in the end I'll have you to myself. I always get what I want. Now, is there anything else I should know about you, Princess Pine?"

"You call me that again and I'll remove a very sensitive part of your body. That I can guarantee you."

He chuckles as he kisses along my neck. My head tips to the side on instinct to grant him better access. The soft groan he makes causes a shiver to rush through me. His hands skim over my back, then to my sides, and up to the bottom of my breasts, where his thumbs gently caress the underside. I arch my back and start to grind against him. I can feel him harden beneath me. I'm not usually so brazen. There's something about him. I let go of everything and simply enjoy this time. He nips along my shoulder, but eventually shifts back.

"Why did you stop?" I ask breathily.

"Because when I take you, and I will take you, it will be in my bed with no rush. I'll take my time discovering every curve of your body. I'll find out how you taste everywhere. I'll make you scream my name in pleasure, and then you'll be mine. You'll confess you have feelings for me, eventually."

I bite my lower lip and look away from him. Truth be told, I do feel something for him. Something so deep it scares me. It's not normal to feel so much, so fast. I know this, but I can't deny the way my body reacts to his nearness, or how being in his arms seems right. I've never felt anything close to this with my ex and that's not lost on me.

We spend the rest of the day inside Luke's home. He doesn't want to go outside until his brothers and sister get the chance to meet me and find out everything from his father. Even though there are people in the kingdom who've seen me, and us hold hands, he said he'd rather not add fuel to gossip that's already spreading.

A guard comes to Luke's home to collect us for dinner. This time I know I don't need to bring my backpack with me. I won't be leaving. Not by force and not to go back home. I'm torn about how I feel, but know I made the right decision. I grab the instructions I've written, and hand-in-hand, Luke and I walk to see the king. There are a few prying eyes who look at us speculatively, but no one says anything to us.

When we enter the dining room, there's a feast spread out before us. My eyes dance over all of the delicious looking food, while my stomach rumbles in anticipation. The king is standing in the corner with two men and a woman in front of him. When he takes notice of our entrance, the other three heads swivel in our direction.

My eyes are first drawn to a man who is the same height as the king, and only a few inches taller than Luke. That's where the differences end between the three of them. This man has dark blond hair and a clean shaven face. His facial structure isn't as angular as Luke's. He takes after Rya. I can see it clear as day, down to his hazel eyes.

We approach them; all of their eyes are drawn to our joined hands.

"It must be true then, brother," the blond man states.

"What are you speaking of, Ry?" Luke replies.

"You've finally found a woman."

His lips quirk up. "It would appear so."

King Azure interjects, "This is Princess Alison

Pine." I hear sharp intakes of breath. "Alison, I would like you to meet my other children, Ryland, Elliott, and Addison." He gestures to each person as he speaks their name. The blond is Ryland. I remember that he'll be the one who will take over the throne.

"Pine?" Ryland asks shocked.

"Yes, Pine," Luke confirms with hardness in his voice and a steel grip on my hand.

"Well, if this isn't an interesting turn of events," Addison comments and starts a slow parade around Luke and me. Her long chestnut hair hangs in soft curls to her mid back. She's wearing black cotton pants like the men, but her shirt is a deep maroon v-neck that accentuates her breasts. "Of all of my brothers I never thought it would be you," she directs to Luke, "who would stray with the enemy. My ruthless, cut men down at their knees, brother, and he's currently holding hands with Pine's daughter. Whom, mind you, none of us ever knew existed."

I glance at Luke and see his eyes have narrowed considerably. His jaw is set hard. I decide it's my turn to speak, since King Azure doesn't seem quick to jump in.

"I may be Pine's daughter," I confirm. "But I'm not one of his pawns. I have never met the man. My allegiance doesn't lie with him. It lies with Luke and him alone. I know nothing of this kingdom, but I'm one of you now. An equal."

Addison stops directly in front of me with wide eyes. "How dare you speak to us that way! You are not an equal. You are the enemy," she seethes.

I step toe-to-toe with her. "Don't mistake my ignorance about how things work here for weakness. I'm not afraid of you, and I will not be spoken to like I am a lesser a person." I'm royalty. It's time to act like it, even if it means being a bitch to people. I'm not going to allow anyone to walk all over me and condemn Luke for standing by my side. Screw that.

I quickly dart my eyes at Luke's brothers. Ryland has a look of indifference, and I'm waiting for Elliott to burst out laughing. He appears to be seconds away from completely losing it. His lips are twitching and his eyes are crinkling at the corners. He's almost the same height as Luke and has light brown hair. His eyes are the same hazel color as Ryland.

Elliott steps forward and offers his hand to me, breaking the tension between Addison and me. I take it in mine. He bows at the waist and kisses the back of my hand. "It's a pleasure to meet you, Princess Alison." He stands and his gaze flickers between Luke and me. "I apologize for the behavior of my sister. I would say she isn't normally so rude, but that would be a lie. This is Addi's normal behavior. Love her or hate her, she is who she is."

Addison rolls her eyes behind him. "No surprise Elliott sides with our baby brother." She backs a few steps away from me.

King Azure finally interrupts, "Enough. There is a reason I've summoned all of you here and before you even question it, Addison, Princess Alison has every right to be at our table, as you do." Addison whips around and gives her father an incredulous stare. "Sit. Now. All of you."

Ryland sits on one side of the king, Luke on the other with me beside him. Elliott sits beside me and Addison is directly across from me, throwing daggers my way. We all begin to eat and the king starts his talk, or confession, if you will.

I pretend my food is the most fascinating thing in the world as he starts his story with me arriving at the cottage. He goes into how I found out about their land. How I'm the daughter of King Pine, yet know nothing of him. That Oliver is supposed to be my future husband. Then he dives into the real heart of the discussion: Rya. How she's very alive and when she left she was pregnant. I lift my head to watch their reaction to the news that their mother is alive. Elliott has almost the same reaction as Luke did. Addison is sitting still with tears streaming down her cheeks, and Ryland remains stoic, showing no emotion.

Then he gets to the pivotal part about the key and how he's using it to go in search of her. How I gave him the key and sacrificed my ability to go home, so he can possibly bring her back. One by one their heads turn to me. I drop my eyes to my plate again, although I can still feel the heat of their stares on me.

All the while, Luke's hand remains in mine. He doesn't let go until Elliott reaches for me and pulls me into his arms. I hold him back as he whispers in my ear, his voice thick with emotion. "Thank you. Thank you for coming here and giving my father the opportunity to find my mother. And thank you for accepting my brother." I pull back to take in his expression. He smiles softly. "I doubt Luke has told you, but he never lets women close to him. Not even as a child. Once mom died, or left rather, he only befriended boys and as he got older, men. Sure, he's been in bed with many women—"

"Elliott!" Luke yells from behind me.

Elliott laughs, but continues, "All I mean is that no woman has been let inside his caged heart. He keeps himself closed off. To see him holding your hand and standing with you, it's...well, it's amazing. I, for one, am very happy to have you here with us." He then pushes his chair back and kneels before me. I have no idea what's going on and turn to Luke, whose eyes soften.

"I, Elliott Azure, as second-in-command of the Azure Elite, pledge myself to protect you. I also pledge my loyalty to you and will stand by your side, as my brother does." He stands and peers down at me. "I can never repay all that you've given up for us, but I'll try."

My eyes mist over and I shake my head. "You

don't have to do that. It's the least I can do. If it were the other way around, I'd want someone to help me get my mother back." A tear escapes and glides down my cheek. "I'd give anything to have my mom with me, even for one day."

I turn to look at the family in front of me. I settle on King Azure and reach into my pocket to get the instructions I wrote out. Standing, I walk over to hand him the paper. "Take this with you. Read it tonight before you leave in the morning. Ask me any questions you have, no matter the time. I want to be sure you're as prepared as possible for crossing over to my world. It's nothing like it is here. The town you will step into is very small and the people very friendly, but I advise you stay in my apartment until Rya can get to you. There is food and everything you could need except clothes."

He takes the paper, then stands and embraces me. It's the last thing I expect and remain frozen. Pulling back, his hands grip my upper arms and he says, "Thank you. This will never be forgotten." I nod and return to my seat.

The scary king I met only yesterday, turned into the warm, kind man before me. What a difference a day makes. Yesterday, I was thrown into a dungeon. Today, I'm welcomed as part of the family, at least by some.

King Azure starts speaking again, but this time it's business. He's going over what they will tell their people and how Ryland will be in charge until, if and when, he returns. After all, we don't know what the key will do once he's on the other side. It's old magic and could decide its work is done. There's no way to tell.

CHAPTER ELEVEN

Speech

It's late; at least I think it is, by the time we get back to Luke's home. I shower and throw on another one of his t-shirts. I'm out of clean clothes now. I only had the two outfits with me. He tells me that tomorrow, once we see King Azure off with his brothers and sister, we'll go to the local clothing vendor to get some clothes for me. He said I can dress however I like; pants, dresses, it doesn't matter since I'm royalty. I still think it's crap that women of lower standing wear dresses only, but this world is also very different than mine.

The Azures have decided to say that the king is going away on a secret mission, and Ryland will be in charge in his absence. Ryland will address the people tomorrow, and he'll also publicly welcome me into their kingdom. King Azure told me to be prepared for backlash, but with the royal family behind me, that should help minimize it. They are going to say I only recently found out who my father is, but I will ally with the Azures and not Pine.

I crawl into bed and pull the damask closed. It's odd to have this heavy fabric draped around the bed. It makes me feel safe, though. Like I'm wrapped up in my own little world with Luke. In a way we are, at least until reality comes knocking on the door again.

Snuggled beneath the blankets, my eyes close, and I start to drift off to sleep when a warm body slides into bed behind me. His scent envelopes me as his arms do the same. Reaching up, I hold tight to his hands. There's something very comforting about him. I won't admit this out loud yet, but he feels like home. Each hour I'm here, this place works its way into my very essence. I'm becoming comfortable here: in Luke's bed, in his arms, and in his kingdom.

He brushes my hair aside, so he can feather kisses along my neck. "Tomorrow is going to be a long day."

I scoff. "Like today wasn't?"

"Okay, well tomorrow might be longer. We have to see my father off before first light. Only the Elite knows of his departure. It will be us, them, and my brothers and sister. Then we have to address the public."

"Fun," I say sarcastically.

"Sleep, my princess. Tomorrow is a new day."

"Yeah, a long one apparently."

He laughs in between kisses below my ear. His grip tightens as he brings himself close to me. Together we drift off into sleep. A sleep where I have no dreams, only restful peace.

———————————◆———————————

It's been a whirlwind since I woke up. We left under moonlight with the Azure family and the eight members of the Elite, Luke and Elliott complete the ten Elite. We said goodbye to the king before he used the key to enter my world. Addison fought tears, Elliott embraced his father, Luke did the same, and Ryland said farewell with a handshake. I don't understand him in the least, however the king and Luke feel strongly he will be an excellent leader in King Azure's absence. It was understood that Luke is to maintain control of the Elite and the king's army. All directions in regard to protection and defense fall to him.

At first light, the members of the army were put to work gathering all of the locals to the courtyard for an announcement. I stood with the Azures as Ryland vaguely spoke of his father's mission, and how nothing will change, except for the fact that he is their interim ruler. My palms are sweating. I keep wiping them on my pants. Black pants that Addison let me borrow. We aren't the same size. I'm taller and leaner, however cotton is flexible and works for now. She also gave me a top to wear, one she made sure to say that she didn't wear anymore. How I can't wait for this to be over so I can get my own clothes.

"Now on to other business," Ryland speaks. "You may have noticed the woman standing beside my brother, Lucas. Some of you have seen them together since she arrived a couple of days ago. I'd like to take this opportunity to introduce you to Princess Alison Pine." Gasps are heard throughout the crowd. Some women's hands fly up to cover their mouths. Men narrow their eyes at me. I'm honestly waiting for someone to hand out pitchforks and torches like one of the old movies I used to watch.

"Quiet," Ryland commands. "Do not judge the princess due to her name. You know nothing of her." It's surprising that he's standing up for me. I don't get the warm and fuzzy vibe from him.

"And you do?" someone calls from the crowd.

"I know enough," he responds. "She will be living within our walls as part of our royal family. While she may hold the Pine name, she is not one of them. She has demonstrated her loyalty to our king and to our family."

"In what way?" another person shouts.

"That is official business and I will not be divulging the details. Just know she is our friend and ally. I demand you treat her with the same respect as you do me and my family. If I hear of any dissonance amongst our people due to her presence, it will be dealt with swiftly and without hesitation by our Elite. A move against the princess is a move against the royal family. Do I make myself clear?" People nod; some never move. I can feel their burning hatred of me. It will take a while for me to gain their trust. At least I know being alongside Luke, I'll be safe.

He steps closer to me and takes my hand in his. Some people don't react to the gesture. They must have been the ones who've seen us together. Others gasp again, and if I'm not mistaken some women give me the evil eye. Ryland turns toward us and nods to Luke. It's his turn to speak.

"Nothing changes in regards to the protection of our kingdom," he says loudly. "Our elite forces, as well as our army, will maintain peace within our land. To follow-up on my brother's words, a move against the princess is a move against me, and you know I don't play games. This woman beside me is kind, gentle, and someone who is very important to me. Do not disrespect her, in or out of our presence."

Addison steps forward. "You've been given a lot of news today, and I understand how this will have upset some of you. Our king is gone for the time being, and an enemy's daughter is living amongst us. But be sure, we are a unified front. The words my brothers have spoken go for Elliott and myself as well, our king, too. Before he left for his mission, he embraced Princess Alison along with the rest of our family. Treat her as our own and we won't have any problems." She turns and nods to Ryland, who concludes the speech.

The crowd disperses, but not before some rake their eyes over me in disgust. Luke catches it and moves himself in front of me to glower down at them. They quickly leave like dogs with their tails between their legs.

He turns and cradles my face in his hands. "It's over now. We can move forward. You're no longer the hidden secret." In relief, I let out the breath I'm holding. He presses his lips to mine in a tender kiss. A throat clearing breaks us apart. We both look over to see Elliott watching us with a big grin on his face.

"Luke's in love," he singsongs. Luke lunges for him so fast, he doesn't have a chance to get away. He's got super-human strength. He grabs Elliott around the neck in a chokehold and holds him tight to his side.

"What did you say?" Luke asks him.

"You heard me, little brother."

"I'm not so little right now, am I?" I can tell they're joking around. They both have smiles on their faces while they tease one another. It's nice to see them have fun. Everything since I've gotten here has been so serious. Maybe things can calm down now.

"Would you two stop being so immature?" Addison throws over her shoulder as she walks by to leave.

"Never!" Elliott calls. Luke grinds his knuckles into his head and releases him. Elliott takes a step away, then it's his turn to lunge for Luke. They wrestle around for a bit. I stand on the sidelines watching their fun. Addison steps up beside me. I thought she had left.

"You break my brother's heart, and I'll break you," she threatens. "The seers aren't the only one with abilities." I have no idea what she means by this, and know if I ask I won't get an answer.

I look at her, but am not the least bit ruffled by her threat. "I hear you loud and clear. Let's just hope he doesn't break mine either." Her eyes meet mine, surprise evident in them.

"I'm not a bad person, Addison. I'm just trying to find my way through life like everyone else. This world of yours is new to me. I'm doing the best I can. I can't deny the attraction I have toward your brother, nor do I want to. He's my anchor in this realm. My source of calm. He never told you about his dreams, did he?" She shakes her head. I turn back to watch the brothers toss each other around. "We've both been dreaming about the other for a while now. Little did we know that we were starring in each other's dreams. We connected long before I showed up at the cottage. We're joined, he and I, on a level I never imagined possible." Just then Luke looks up and graces me with a megawatt smile that makes my stomach flutter.

"I had no idea," she admits quietly.

"I trust that we can keep this between us."

"Yes, of course." I have a feeling the hard ass attitude I've been getting from her has just changed. Maybe one day we can be friends.

───────◆───────

Luke and I spend the remainder of the morning shopping. We stop by the local clothing vendor so I can pick out enough clothes, bras, and underwear to last me at least a week without having to do laundry. High-end lingerie it's not, but it will have to do. We stroll hand-in-hand through the courtyard, visiting other vendors along the way. He said it might be good for them to see us out and about together, showing them I'm not a threat.

We drop the packages we purchased back at his home. King Azure made sure that I have access to my own money and a lot of it, at that. I can't imagine ever needing that much money. However, he told me if I ever run out, his children are to give me more. They're to keep me set for life. It makes me wonder just how wealthy they are.

I drop down on the couch, exhausted from the day's events, and close my eyes. Luke sits beside me, but before he can get settled there's a knock on the door. I open my eyes and stand. He strides to the door and opens it, speaking with whoever is on the other side in a hushed voice. Then I see his shoulders tighten, but he takes a step back, allowing the person in.

An older woman steps in. She has beautiful, straight silver hair that falls to her mid-back. She's petite and curvy. Her navy twill pants accentuate her hips, as does her white, long-sleeved blouse. It's light and airy. Her eyes are the same silver as her hair. They captivate me and draw me in.

I step toward her. She smiles. Her eyes sparkle from the sunlight being let in by the still open door. Luke closes it behind her and offers her a seat in his living area. She sits in one of the chairs across from the couch where Luke and I sit.

"Alison, this is Stephanie. She's a seer. Our only one. She asked to speak with you."

"It's nice to meet you."

"You too, Alison Wescot," she replies. Her voice is like a melody. I'm taken aback by her knowing my name, but then again, I'm assuming she probably knows everything about me.

Luke slides closer to me and takes my hand in his. I've noticed that when there are people around us, he presses to my side. I'm not sure if it's him staking his claim on me, or if he's letting the person know I'm protected by him. Either way, I take comfort in the warmth of his hand and his thigh pressed to mine.

"What would you like to talk to the princess about?" Luke inquires.

"Well, I was going to ask to speak to her alone, but I know you better than that, Your Highness. You aren't going to let this woman out of your sight. Not now, or ever."

Luke nods and then she looks at me. "Alison, my dear, I came to warn you. King Pine is coming, and he's prepared to wage a war to get you."

CHAPTER TWELVE

Warning

"I don't want him to fight anyone to speak with me," I reply.

"He doesn't want to speak. The king knows where your allegiance lies and wants you on his side. I'm not the only seer in the realm. He has his own advisors. How do you think he found out you were here?"

"I won't side with him. I belong here, with Luke, and the rest of the Azures." It's the truth. This man, who I've never met, dares to threaten these people with war. No, I will not side with him.

"My visions can change, my dear. They change due to your decisions. You have the ability to stop a war before it starts."

Luke stands abruptly. "I won't let her go with him. Or with Sage," he growls.

"Easy, young prince. I didn't say she would have to go with him, but her actions are the catalyst. Everything hinges on her and how she and you respond," she replies pointedly.

He rakes his hand through his hair. "What do we do? How do I keep her safe, and here, without causing war? Although, I would love a chance at him. If it weren't for the potential loss of life, I'd let him bring a war to our borders. It would be my pleasure to cut him down." I cringe at his words. The idea of Luke being the killer, which Oliver told me about, is nothing I want to ever witness. It's bad enough in my head, let alone seeing it in real life.

"Your Highness," Stephanie addresses him in a calm tone. "Take a seat. You're startling the princess." He peers down at me and his eyes soften. Sitting by my side, he takes my hands in his again and looks at me with an apology clearly written all over his face.

"You need to remember, Prince Lucas, Alison isn't of our world. Our ways are not her own. It's going to take her a bit to get used to everything. She has a kind heart and is a peacemaker by nature. Yes, she will stand up for herself or those she loves, but she'd much prefer not to fight or argue. If you care for her, you'll remember this when in her presence. She's heard about you and what you've done. Be easy with your words."

Luke drops his gaze from mine and hangs his head. I turn to the seer and chastise her. "Don't make him feel guilty for being himself and protecting those in his kingdom. Yes, I've heard he's a killer, but I bet many men in this realm are. Do I want a war? No, especially not because of me. Now tell me what I can do to prevent it?"

She seems unfazed by my outburst. "King Pine will not rest until he's laid his eyes on you and spoken with you. His ultimate goal is to bring you to his side, but I think you can appease him, for now, if you meet and talk to him."

"No!" Luke shouts. "He could kill her if she were to meet with him in person."

"That is why you and Prince Elliott will be by her side. Also, as much as you and Oliver Sage have hatred toward one another, he would never allow the king to harm her. He would lay his life down for her, even if it meant going against his ruler. Yes, he's a fighter, but he has a soft spot for her."

"He doesn't even know me," I interrupt.

Stephanie smiles. "Like I said, this world isn't the same as yours. You were promised to him many years ago. Just because he never met you, doesn't mean he doesn't care for you. Oliver has lived his life waiting for his chance."

"He didn't even know I existed."

"He didn't? King Pine has seers, remember. Oliver knew you were out there and was biding his time until you came to meet your father. I don't believe his feelings are on the same level as your prince here, but if you choose a life with him, he would spend his days putting you first and living to make you happy."

How can someone who doesn't know me feel this way? It doesn't make any sense, but then again I'm talking to someone who can look into the future.

"Wait a minute," Luke interrupts. "How do you know how Alison will be treated by Sage? You've seen her future with him?" Is that jealousy I hear in his voice? Does he think I'll choose Oliver over him? I thought I made my intentions known when I said I'd like to stay here with him.

"The future isn't certain. Princess Alison can select which path she walks down. I've seen both futures, one with you and one with Oliver. Only she can choose. Not me. Not you. But we're getting off-topic. I came here with a warning and now must go. There is a lot for you to do and prepare for. King Pine will be at our borders in two week's time.

"He's giving you some time, Princess. He believes Prince Lucas will show you a side of himself that will make you want to leave. He doubts how genuine Luke is with you around. He's also preparing his army for battle. I suggest you do the same. The Azure Army is the strongest around. They need to be prepared to face their opponent. Even if the princess agrees to meet with him, his men will be lying in wait. It would be foolish not to have your own men standing behind you."

She stands and we follow. Stepping close to me, she clasps my free hand in both of hers. Her eyes twinkle in delight. "It's truly been a pleasure meeting you. You're a phenomenal woman, and I know the best is yet to come. Always remain true to yourself and follow your instincts. Everything else will fall into place." I nod and squeeze her hand. Luke escorts her outside. I hear him talking, but can't make out the words. As I inch closer, he returns.

He walks to me and I can see the hesitation in his eyes. His arms lift slightly, although fall back to his side. His hands form fists. I know he wants to hold me, but he's unsure. Stephanie said a lot in the short time she was here. I bet he's wondering if I want to be with Oliver. I need to ease his turmoil.

I close the space between us. Lifting my hand, I rub my thumb over the stubble on his cheek. "Luke, if I wanted to be with Oliver I wouldn't spend the night with you. I'm not that type of woman. I don't mess around with different men. If I'm here with you, then it's only you. I'm not even thinking of other men." Taking a deep breath, I get ready to admit something I've been keeping to myself. "You've held a piece of my heart since the first dream we shared. Every dream since, you've had me yearning for your touch. Now that I've slept with your arms around me, and felt your lips on my own, I can't walk away. Please trust me when I say I don't want to be with Oliver. I don't want to live in my father's kingdom. I do want to meet him, though, especially if it can help prevent war. I want to know the man who my mother fell in love with. I need to."

His shoulders lose their tension and he rests his forehead on mine. "Ali, you have no idea how much your words mean to me. Seeing you with Sage would kill me. You're mine and have been since that first dream."

He captures my lips with his. There's a possessive heat to his kiss. His hands grip my hips, bringing me flush against him. Why can't I just get lost in his touch and not think about all that could go wrong? I know I need to meet with my father, but what if something happens, and Luke gets hurt? Or Elliott or one of his men? I don't want that resting on my shoulders.

I break away from him. "I need to speak with my father. I have to do everything I can to prevent your kingdoms from going to war."

"I don't like it. You could be hurt. He could capture you and take you from me."

"You heard Stephanie. It needs to be done."

"She also said the future changes."

"She did, and I want to change it for the better, not the worse. I need to do this."

Two weeks fly by in the blink of an eye. Luke and I have grown closer. We haven't crossed the line into sex yet, but damn it's been hard to hold out. He insists we wait, and even though I'm growing impatient, I know it's the right thing. Every day I give another tiny piece of my heart to him. Every day I fall deeper under his spell.

Ryland received word, a few of days ago, that my father is expecting him to turn me over to him this morning along with Oliver Sage, or to be prepared to face his wrath. A messenger was sent back saying the Azure family stands with me and that no one would be handing me over. Ryland did convey that there could be a meeting where I'll get to speak with my father. He also said Oliver would be released back to King Pine as a show of good faith. He doesn't want to start a war, but if need be, the Azures are prepared for battle. My father agreed to the meeting, and in kind, will be handing over the Azure prisoners he has within his walls.

Stephanie visited shortly after we got word that he agreed. She said the king knows I'm my own person, however will be doing everything he can to sway me to his side. By him releasing the men he has as prisoners, he's hoping I'll see he's a good man. She said we also need to be prepared, in case he tries to capture me. There is some uncertainty with her vision, and she stressed for us to be on guard, which worries me.

I've been given a short sword and taught basic

moves by Elliott. Luke has been busy preparing the Elite and the army. We'll be taking the Elite and some army soldiers with us to our meeting, as per Stephanie's suggestion. The Elite will be arriving on their dragons, including me with Luke. The other men headed out early this morning on horseback, along with Oliver Sage. There aren't enough dragons in the kingdom for all of the men. Luke explained that most battles are held on the ground, but he needs to be sure he can get me out of there quickly if he has to. The Elite will surround and protect us until we are back safely within the walls of the castle.

Twice this past week, I've gone on flights with Luke and Tali. Both were at night and each time I was more at ease on her. She seems to like me better, even greeting me first last time, instead of Luke.

We're currently making our way to the building where the dragons are kept. I'm dressed in black pants and an azure top. I had no idea you could dye a fabric the exact color of a flower. My shirt is proof. It was Luke's idea. He said he wanted King Pine to see where I stand, and that I have no intention of going with him. He said my father would be doing all he could to sway me, so why not play dirty as well, and show up in azure.

Luke is dressed in full armor. You know how when you read books where there's a knight in shining armor, and you imagine how he would look? Well, I can tell you that your imagination could never do justice to the real thing. The man walking beside me, with his hand on the small of my back, looks like a force to be reckoned with. It's sexy as hell. I almost became a puddle on the floor when he first stepped into my line of sight this morning.

His hair is combed back from his face, his beard has grown a little fuller, but he still keeps it neat. The armor is a brilliant steel blue. It magnifies the intensity of his blue eyes. There's an eagle on the breastplate with its talons spread wide and feathers sticking out on either side. The eagle is the symbol for the Azure Kingdom. On his right arm is a lion, which he told me represents the elite group he leads. There is a matching steel blue cape that billows behind him while he walks at my side. I can't keep my eyes off of him. I'm surprised I haven't walked into anything yet from lack of paying attention. The way the armor molds to his body does very wicked things to me.

He stops in front of the door where the dragons are. I almost run smack into it. Luke chuckles. "You really should watch where you're going," he says with mirth.

"I can't help it when you look like that."

He reaches an arm around my waist and draws me to him; my chest presses close to the cold of his armor. His lips claim mine and the world falls away. It's only Luke and me in the moment. The way he holds me tenderly. The way his lips and tongue move with my own. I really wish we didn't have this whole potential war hanging over our heads.

145

Luke breaks our kiss first. "We need to get going. They're waiting for us."

It takes a minute for my mind to clear. I look around and see the members of Luke's Elite watching us. They're each dressed in the same armor. Elliott is leaning against the building with a wide smile. I blush and bury my face against Luke. The cold metal of his armor, and the men staring at us, effectively puts a damper on my far from innocent thoughts.

Luke places his arm across my shoulders and leads us into the building first. Each man finds and brings out his dragon. We all go outside to the cliff we will soon jump from. Elliott positions his dragon in front of Tali. His dragon is black as night. All of the other dragons range in color from green to red. Luke's is the only white one and Elliott's is the only midnight one. My guess is it's just another way to distinguish status amongst the warriors. Luke explained that he normally leads his men, but since he will have me with him, Elliott is taking the lead spot to provide further defense.

We climb on Tali's back and I'm surprised with the agility Luke has in the armor. He says it's due to practicing with his men while wearing it. They try to get as used to it as possible. Although, he said he would rather not wear any. I gave him the evil eye when he told me that and said he needs to keep it on and keep himself safe. He smiled, however didn't say anything further.

I notice the change in Tali's demeanor. Normally she nuzzles me and seems equally as curious about me as I am of her. Today she's completely focused on the task at hand. Her eyes are thin, amethyst slits, her body taut, she's poised for what's to come.

My stomach drops as she dives from the cliff. Squeezing my eyes shut, I hug her neck. Luke has one protective arm around the front of my waist, but I still hold on for dear life. When we even out, I open my lids and see the other dragons have formed a protective circle around us. I don't think I'm worth all of the extra protection, but Luke insists. He said that I'm treated as anyone in the royal family would be.

This is no leisurely flight through the sky. We're going faster than ever before and are flying straight ahead. Straight toward my father.

CHAPTER THIRTEEN

King Pine

Out in the distance the Pine castle looms, and there are men on the ground below us. Tali is making wide circles while half of the Elite land. Elliott is already on the ground and signals it's clear for us to land as well. Tali's feet hit the grass gracefully, but she hangs back from the line the other dragons on the ground have formed. The rest of the men drop behind us to keep us surrounded. Half dismount, half stay on. The members of the army are standing in front of the dragons. They're the first defense. It's amazing to see the seamless formation of the men. No words are spoken, they all know what to do.

Luke jumps down from Tali first and holds out his hand to help me. We slowly walk to the front of the line. Luke is one side of me, while Elliott flanks the other. Both of their faces are hard, and I can see why so many are afraid of Luke. He doesn't scare me, though. He and Elliott provide me great comfort knowing they're on my side.

When the army parts to allow us through, the other few Elite men, who left their dragons, are with us. Luke had told me there are a few contingency plans in case something goes wrong. He didn't provide me with any details. He only said that no matter what I'll be taken care of. But what if something happens to him or his men? Who will take care of them? That thought has been circling in my mind since he told me there are plans.

With the sun shining brightly above, I shield my eyes to look in front of me. As we step closer, towering pine trees block out some of the rays and allow me to see better. We are officially on the border of the two kingdoms.

Standing directly in front of me is a man who makes me falter in my steps. He looks exactly like me: same dark hair and slender nose, tall and thin, but he's in armor. It's an evergreen color with the head of a wolf on front. He's the exact height as me. I can't help but stare. I notice he's doing the same thing. His mouth is hanging open as he takes me in. This is my brother, Reid. He lunges forward, but before he reaches me, Luke shoots out his arm and hits him in the throat. Elliott swiftly moves me behind him, however I shift to peer around him to see what's going on.

Reid stumbles back grasping his throat. Men from the other side advance as does the Azure Army. They're standing toe-to-toe. I start to shake, unsure of what's going to happen. I've lost Luke in the mix and only see a wall of men and Elliott in front of me.

"Enough!" a loud voice bellows. "Stand down. All of you."

"We don't take commands from you," I hear Luke seethe. He's still close.

"I was talking to my own men, but I suggest your men back off as well."

"We will do no –"

"Luke," Elliott interrupts from his place before me. Then I see him. My Prince and defender. The man who makes my stomach flutter in excitement and can knock someone down with one look. The man, who people fear, but also look up to within his own kingdom. The man who every night wraps me tight in his embrace and remains there until I wake.

Over the past two weeks we've grown closer. So close, I started calling him mine as he has done from the beginning with me. He turns to look at his brother and then his eyes fall on me. They soften a bit. He knows Elliott kept me safe. I take a step forward and Luke meets me in the middle, while Elliott walks around him to ensure Luke's back isn't left unguarded. These two move fluidly with one another.

Luke looks down at me and places a gentle kiss

on my nose. "Are you ready?" he asks quietly.

I can only nod. I'm not ready. Nowhere close to it, but time waits for no one, and I need to finally meet my father. Luke's hand protectively settles on my back as he brings me forward with him. We pass the line of the Azure Army and stop beside Elliott. There is a tall, imposing figure in front of me. He has dark red hair and a long, matching beard. He's in armor that matches Reid's and is wide like a linebacker.

I stop a few feet from him. Luke and Elliott are with me, and at some point, Oliver joined us along with one of the other Elite. Reid has regained his composure and is standing beside our father. They look nothing alike.

"My daughter finally comes home," the king states with a smile, but this is not a warm, welcoming smile. No. It's one of triumph. He must think I'm here to go with him.

My fear begins to melt away and my resolve builds. Maybe it's all of the strong men around me. Maybe it's the strength I'm borrowing from Luke, since he seems to have enough for ten men. I'm not sure where it comes from, but I'm going to harness it and use it to speak with my father. The man who has been absent all of my life.

I square my shoulders and raise my chin. "Your definition of home is different than mine. While the Pine Kingdom is yours, my home is with the Azures."

His lips thin and he speaks with serious tone. "Your home is with me and your brother. Your home is with your destined husband, Oliver."

"No," I say, shaking my head. "I have a choice, and I choose to stay with the Azures. I choose to be with Luke. I will not be forced into a marriage with a man I don't know nor love."

"You're foolish. You don't know what you're giving up."

"I'm giving nothing up, only gaining everything I've always wanted."

Reid takes a hesitant step forward while still rubbing his neck. "Alison, I didn't mean to startle you before. I'm sorry. I was surprised by how alike we look and was going to embrace you. I've wanted to meet you for so long. I can't believe you're finally standing in front of me. Please, come with us. I'd love to get to know you."

"I can get to know you without living within your walls. We can meet and talk, but on neutral ground."

"Whatever you'd like."

I give him a small smile, but bring my eyes back to my father. "I want you to turn over the men of the Azure Army in exchange for Oliver."

"Fair enough, daughter. I'm a man of my word." He waves his hand and two men come forward with guards on either side of them. Oliver, however, doesn't look like he knows where to go. He stands in the middle of the lines.

He turns to me with pleading eyes. "Please, Princess. Come home with me. I will care for you and make you happy. Anything your heart desires, I will provide. Please."

My heart breaks a little for him. He was nice to me down in the dungeon on my first day here, and from what Stephanie said, he only has the best intentions where I'm concerned. However, I'm not his and will never be. My heart belongs to another.

"Oliver," I say, stepping closer to him and placing my hand on his arm. I notice Luke and Elliott move with me. "I can't. I'm sorry. My place is beside Luke. I know my father promised my hand to you, but he never should have. I'm a woman who has her own mind. I don't do as I'm told. I was raised by a mother," I look to Reid briefly, "who taught me to be an individual, to never let someone dictate my life. She made me strong and gave me confidence to believe in myself. Things that Luke and the rest of the Azures embrace about me. They don't try to mold me into something I'm not. I can't be who you want me to. You wouldn't be happy with the woman I am."

"I would," Oliver quickly states. "I'll love you the rest of our lives for who you are. I don't want to change you, only to have you in my life."

Shaking my head, I say, "I can't go with you. I'm sorry." His eyes close and my heart hurts a little more.

"Move aside, Sage," my father demands. He pushes Oliver and stands directly in front of me. Oliver falters for a second, but then places himself between my father and me. Luke and Elliott have stepped forward, blocking me as well. A wall of strength.

Luke growls, "Take one more step, Pine, and I will slit your throat just like I did to your second in command. You remember him, don't you? The one you sent to fight me, since you were too cowardly. Yet, you cut down Leo with no problem. I don't know whether you're stupid or have a death wish. Either way, I'm happy to grant the wish."

"Afraid? Of you?" My father starts laughing a big, hearty laugh. "That's rich."

Luke moves until he's nose-to-nose with my father. Oliver doesn't stray from his position in front of me. He appears to be protecting me, but I'm not completely sure. I know he wants me as his, and my father wants me to come with him. Maybe they are doing this to take me. At this point I only can trust Luke and the Azures. The Pine Army moves to stand beside their leader. Reid is swallowed up by them, pushed to the back and out of my sight.

"Enough of the games. Sage, get over here and bring my daughter with you," my father commands.

Oliver doesn't move. I look around and everyone appears to be ready to jump into battle. Then a loud roar punctures the sky and everyone, including me, turns toward the sound. Oliver now stands next to me to see where it came from. Tali has her head pointed high and is roaring almost piercingly. Her front legs lift from the ground. She must have sensed the tension in the air.

I look to Oliver, but before I get a word out, I'm jolted back against a hard chest of armor. The metal chills my skin through my shirt. A cold blade bites into the skin of my neck. I freeze on the spot. I can already feel something warm run down my neck, and know if I move further, the wound will be much worse.

Looking around, I see a look of pure shock on Oliver's face. Elliott has his sword drawn along with everyone else in the Azure Army and the Elite. They must have been watching Tali along with me and my father stepped up behind me. I was vulnerable and he took advantage of it. I glance around wildly trying to locate Luke without moving my head. I don't see him anywhere. How can he be gone when I need him most?

"Father, don't do this," Reid begs. He's only a couple of feet away now. "You need to stop this. Let her go." My father is the one who's trying to harm me. The man who my mother told me to find and that I'd be safe with. He must have been a different man when she knew him. She never would have told me to find someone who would try to hurt me.

"Wouldn't you love that, my son? You're always

trying to avoid conflict. You spend more time smoothing things over between people in our land than addressing the real problems."

"To our people, their issues are real. To them they're not insignificant like you think they are. They need my help and I'm happy to provide it. I don't want this war. Alison said what she wanted. Let it be."

"You're weak. You always have been. Just like your mother. She couldn't handle battle either and fled when it got bad."

Reid's face becomes as hard as the armor he wears. "Did you ever consider it wasn't the war she was running from? Maybe it was you?"

My father's grip on me tightens at Reid's words. "How dare you speak to me that way!" he bellows.

"Let her go." Oliver demands in a low and deadly voice. His sword is drawn, and he's pointing it at us, or at my father to be more precise. The sword hovers higher than my shoulder toward my father's head.

"You too, Sage? I should have known. Ever since you found out I had a daughter, you've become obsessed with finding her."

A loud, deep voice yells, "Free her now or suffer the consequences, Pine!" Luke. He's somewhere amidst the army, but I can't find him.

The blade cuts deeper into my skin and I gasp in fear. A tear runs down my cheek. Elliott looks like he's barely able to hold still, and Oliver flashes between fear and murderous rage.

"Show yourself, Azure. I know you're out there. One slip of the wrist and she's dead."

"You'd kill your own blood?" Elliott asks in astonishment. I thought that was obvious, but maybe Elliott thought it was all a ruse.

"Of course. I don't want her in the hands of my enemy to be used against me." I'm nothing to him but a pawn in this messed up game he's playing. A game of lives.

"You're sick," Elliott says.

"King Pine, it doesn't have to be this way," Oliver adds. "You can let her go and walk away."

"Never," my father hisses.

A whooshing sound reaches my ears seconds before there is a loud thump behind me. My father gasps in my ear, and I hear Luke speak low and cold, "Never try to take from me what's mine."

The blade at my neck slides and slices deeper. Elliott rushes forward and grasps my father's arm to pull him away from me. The coldness at my back is gone. I fall into Elliott's arms, blood trickling down my neck. I turn around to see Luke standing there with a bloody knife in his hand. My father is lying on his side, on the ground, with a growing pool of crimson beneath him. His chest rises once, twice, he coughs out blood and grows still. No more breaths.

My hand flies to my mouth and I look at Luke. He lowers his head and turns away from me. My father is dead. All of my father's men reach for Luke at the same time, but the Elite are there by his side in an instant. Blades start clashing all around me. The ting of each hit rings in my ears. The Azure Army is fighting Pine's.

I start to grow dizzy when strong arms grab me from behind, and I'm lifted in the air. I kick and scream to be let go. I'm unsure who has me and don't want to be held captive. Luke turns at my cries. In the second he meets my eyes, he's left himself unguarded. A blade slashes deeply across his chest and blood starts to seep through his white shirt. He pitches forward, his hand on his chest, but he keeps fighting with his other arm. It's with less force than before.

It's then I realize his armor is gone. Why isn't he wearing it? I'm screaming internally and then externally. "No! Luke! No!" Where's Reid? Why isn't he putting a stop to this? "Reid! You have to stop the fighting!" My eyes scan the area in front of me, and I see him staring down at our father dead on the ground. Reid is immobile. His face is blank. No sadness, no hurt, nothing.

Next thing I know I'm being dragged backward, but not without a struggle. I want to get to Luke. I want to put pressure on his chest. I need him to be okay.

I ball my hands into fists and start punching the

person holding me. Before I know it, I'm being held by two men and placed on a black dragon. We're in the air in seconds. Each sweep of the wings furthers the distance I am from Luke.

"Let me go!" I yell. I don't care who has me at this point. All that matters is returning to Luke.

"We will if you stop struggling," Elliott says from behind me. I turn and give him a death glare. Then I look in front of me and see Oliver. It doesn't even register to me that men of different sides have me.

"We have to go back!" I scream. "How can you leave him there? He's hurt." I turn to look at Elliott again. "He's your brother and you left him! You left him and he needed you."

"I know, Princess. Believe me, I know. But this was the plan. If he got hurt he wanted you taken away at all costs, and that's what we're doing. We have to ensure your safety, and right now you're bleeding. You need to see the healer."

"And what about his safety? Why wasn't he wearing his armor?"

"He's got the rest of the Elite and our army helping him. Also, Luke has a habit of shedding it during battle. He says he can't move as well with it on."

"Why would he do that?" Then I remember him saying how he'd rather not wear any at all. That he's used to it, but still prefers to not have the restriction. "We have to go back!" I cry. Tears start pouring down my cheeks. I grip Oliver's shirt in front of me and sob into him. I don't care that I'm hurt. Luke is all that matters. "Please, we have to go back."

His arms wrap around my back as he pulls me close, but they don't provide the same warmth and comfort that Luke's do. He holds me tightly as the dragon banks to the left, and we make our descent to the Azure Kingdom. Before closing my eyes, I see the field of blue flowers below where I first met my prince.

CHAPTER FOURTEEN

Aftermath

I don't even know how I got from Elliott's dragon to Luke's bed. The healer came to the house to fix me up and left quickly after in anticipation of other casualties. Apparently my wound wasn't as deep as I thought and only needed to be cleaned and bandaged.

I lay in Luke's bed crying for what feels like hours. The last time I felt this helpless was when my mom was dying, and there was nothing I could do to help her. I'm not alone in the room. Oliver has been with me since we landed. Elliott was too for a while. I didn't think he felt comfortable leaving me alone with Oliver, but after the day's events and our location, if Oliver tried to take me he wouldn't get far. Oliver has gotten the brunt of my anger a few times, but I've lost the fight in me. He held me for a while and let me cry on him. I let out all of my fear regarding Luke's well-being. In such a short time, I've become so used to having him around and very attached to him; I don't want to be without him. But it didn't matter how much begging and pleading I did, neither Oliver nor Elliott would let me leave.

The room is dark when a loud disturbance wakes me. I must have dozed off without meaning to. I sit up and see the moon's light shining in, casting a glow upon Oliver. He stiffens near the doorway.

Someone is thumping up the stairs. Wait, two people are. Their voices are a dull murmur and I can't make out who it is. Oliver moves to block the door. Then I hear him. My Prince. He growls, "I may be injured, but I can still kick your ass, Sage. Now move."

My heart is beating wildly. I jump from the bed and am about to shove Oliver out of the way, when he turns to me. The light from downstairs pours in, illuminating his face. Pain is evident in Oliver's eyes, and I hate that I'm the reason it's there. He hangs his head and moves aside.

Luke stumbles in and drops to his knees before me. He looks like hell. His hair is wild, sticking up at odd angles. He's shirtless, only wearing a pair of thin pants. His face is caked with blood, as are his hands, chest, and stomach. I drop to the floor so I'm even with him, and place my hands on his shoulders to steady him as he lists to the side. There are stitches across his chest from the gash I saw earlier. The skin is red and angry.

Moving my hands, I cup his cheeks, bringing his eyes to mine. "Oh, Luke," I whisper. I start to get choked up and try to keep my tears at bay, however it's of no use. Seeing him alive makes me elated, but the blood covering him has me hating that he was hurt because of me.

He sags into my touch. "My princess," he murmurs. "I'm sorry for what I've done. I didn't know what else to do. Please forgive me."

"What are you apologizing for? You didn't do anything wrong. You came back to me. That's all that matters."

His eyes meet mine and I can tell how sincere he is. It occurs to me why he wants forgiveness. He thinks I'm mad that he killed my father. In truth, I never knew the man, and the little bit I saw of him tonight, I'm glad I didn't. How he could hold a sword to his own daughter's neck? I'm not sorry Luke did what he had to so I could be saved. I'm only sorry for all that he endured on my behalf.

"Don't," I say. "You don't have to apologize for that. If you didn't take care of him, then I might not be here."

"He was still your father."

"No," I shake my head. "While I might refer to him that way, he was never a father to me. I gave him the chance to talk to me and he threatened to kill me. A father doesn't do that. A father loves and cherishes their child. He did neither."

Looking up and to my right, I see Elliott and Oliver watching us. "Elliott, please help me get him to the tub. I want to get this blood off of him." He nods and puts one of Luke's arms over his shoulder to gently lift him. I start to follow when I feel a hand on my arm. Turning I see Oliver behind me.

"Princess Alison, I cannot stay here. My kingdom must be in turmoil over the loss of their king. I'd ask you to reconsider joining me, but after the night we've had I don't think there is any way you will." He steps closer, his thumb brushes over my bottom lip. It's too intimate and causes me to lean away. He lets out a sigh. "I know where your heart lies, however should you ever change your mind, I'll be waiting." He leans forward, brushes his lips across my cheek and whispers, "Forever."

"Oliver —"

He doesn't let me finish. "Please, don't say anymore. I want to remember you like this. Beautiful, your eyes only on mine. I don't know when I'll see you again, but should you ever need me, I'm only a short flight away by dragon. I will always come when you request me."

Now there are tears welling in my eyes for a whole different reason. How can someone who doesn't know me, care about me so deeply? I need to tell him that I want him to move on with his life and not wait for me. I'm not the woman for him.

A throat clears behind me, interrupting our conversation. I realize how close Oliver is still standing to me. I take a step back. Oliver's eyes narrow over my shoulder.

"Azure, do you have a horse I can borrow to get back to my kingdom?"

Elliott steps up beside me. He places a protective hand at the small of my back. "I'll do you one better, Sage. I'll let you borrow my dragon. He knows his way back. Plus, if you don't send him back within the hour, I'll come for you," he says with a malicious smile. Oliver nods having gotten the message.

Turning to me, Elliott motions with his head toward the bathroom. I start to walk away, but turn back and close the distance between Oliver and myself. I place a kiss on his cheek and hug him tightly. His arms pull me closer, his cheek resting against mine.

Whispering in his ear, I say, "Thank you for protecting me and ensuring my safety. I'll never forget you, Oliver Sage."

I don't look back when I walk away this time. I can't see the heartache on his face again. I'll splinter open. It's better this way. I don't want to lead him on. The man who holds my heart needs me now.

I step into the bathroom and close the door behind me. Luke is climbing into a tub of water. I've never seen him completely naked before. Even bloody and battered, he's gorgeous. I try the best I can not to focus on his firm ass, or between his legs, when he sinks into the water. I need to get my mind out of the gutter and focus on the task at hand. Not a certain other task I'd like to undertake, and not my hand or mouth performing said task.

I push everything aside in my mind and kneel next to the bathtub, facing him. I find a clean washcloth under the sink and lather it up with a bar of soap. His eyes are closed. His arms are lying on either side of the tub, and his head is resting against the back. I start to wash his neck when his head lifts to watch me. Slowly, I clean his face next, cupping water in my hands to rinse him off, being mindful of his stitches, trying not to get them wet which is proving difficult. I make my way over both arms before cleaning around his wound. Now it's becoming impossible to clean him off and keep the wound dry.

"Why didn't they clean you better when they stitched you up? And why didn't they put a bandage over the stitches?" I ask.

His eyes bore into mine with an intensity I haven't seen yet. "I didn't want another woman touching me, only you. I didn't want you to think I cared for her and that's why I let her touch me."

"She's there to help you, Luke. She needs to touch you to fix you up. If I was there I would have embraced her for doing her best to mend you."

"And she did what she needed, no more. The

stitches were done and I left. I wanted to find you and make sure you were okay. My men wouldn't let me come here first. I tried, but I was quickly overpowered in my weakened state."

"You needed to get that wound closed. I'm glad you got it taken care of. I just wish someone would have told me you were all right."

He chuckles, surprising me. "This," he says, sweeping his arm over his chest, "is nothing. I've been hurt much worse." He lifts his left leg from the water, droplets splashing down, and points to a long scar on the side of his muscular left thigh. I trace it with my finger.

"What happened?"

"The last war was rough on us. A lot were injured, some killed. Someone got the jump on me with their sword and, well, you see the result. It was much deeper than the one on my chest. Walking was not fun for a while. Luckily, it happened at the tail end of the battle, so I didn't miss much of the fight."

"I can imagine you fighting through the pain and continuing on until you fall over."

His lips quirk up on one side. "That's exactly what happened. Elliott had to pull me away from the heat of it and throw me on Tali to get me home. I barely remember the days after. I lost a lot of blood. Elliott said poor Tali looked like she was the one who was stabbed."

I shake my head. "I'm glad I wasn't here to see

it. This is bad enough. I was so scared, Luke. I thought...I thought I wasn't going to see you again." My bottom lip starts to tremble. He reaches up, placing his hand on the back of my neck and pulls me close until our foreheads touch.

"It's going to take a lot more than this to take me away from you. The only way I won't return to your side after a battle is if I'm dead. Hasn't it sunken in yet that I'm yours?"

Placing a gentle kiss on his lips, I pull back and offer a small smile. "It's starting to."

"Finally," he groans. "Your neck. Are you okay?" His fingers trail along the edge of my bandage.

"I'm fine. I didn't need stiches or anything."

"I hate that I couldn't protect you better."

"You did just fine."

I finish cleaning him off and help him get out of the tub, careful to keep my eyes above waist level. Sure, I want to see all of him again now that he's standing up, but I need to behave. He's hurt, exhausted, and in pain. While he won't admit it, I see his mouth pinch tight when he moves.

Finding him shorts, I bring them into the bathroom, and quickly shower while he gets ready for bed. Elliott and Oliver must have left. The house is completely quiet. We both settle into the cool sheets after I draw the damask closed around us, tucking us into our own little cocoon.

He tries to pull me close, but groans in pain, so I gently nudge him onto his back and lay beside him. My leg rests atop his and my fingers settle on his bicep. I don't want to hurt him further.

"Closer," he murmurs groggily.

I scoot as close as possible to his side. "There."

"Not good enough."

"You're hurt and tired. This is as close as I get."

"I hurt more without your body against mine. Now move closer."

I prop myself up on my elbow and try to figure out how to get closer to him without touching his chest. I settle on moving down and placing my head on his stomach while my arm drapes across his hips.

"Not what I had in mind, but much better."

I gently tap his stomach with my hand. "Behave."

He laughs, but then tenses beneath me. The pain must be bad. I tried to get him to take some medicine the healer gave him, although he refused it. I wish he wouldn't be so stubborn. He'd feel better and probably be able to sleep easier.

His body starts to relax beneath me. I take in his warmth and close my eyes. I still don't know how someone I've only known a couple of weeks has gotten under my skin so fast. The fact that I could have lost him today was enough to scare me into thinking of a life without him.

When things started going downhill with my ex, prior to me catching him cheating, my mother confessed she never thought the two of us made sense. I asked her why she never voiced it previously. She asked if I would have listened to her before my wedding day and not gone through with it. I told her no, of course not, and that I loved him regardless of what she had to say I would have married him. Right then I had my answer as to why she never told me.

So, here I lay on a bed, in a house in a faraway land, where dragons fly through the sky, and there is a field of azure flowers. Maybe Luke had a point when he said everything happened the way it did for a reason. If I had dreamt about him earlier in life, would I be where I am right now? Would I have crossed through the portal that day, and if so, would I have given the key to his father so he could go after his mother?

Those questions, and wondering if I'm finally on the right path in life, keep bouncing around my head well into the night. The nap I had earlier didn't do me any favors.

I lift myself from him and lie at his side with my hand on his stomach, so I can feel every breath he takes. I hear his groans of pain when he tries to roll over. I feel his hand seeking me out, attempting to pull me close. Eventually, sleep overcomes me, but I'm left with awful dreams of the battle earlier and the way the blade felt on my neck. Every time I wake gasping for air with my hand flying to my neck. The sting of pain is still there. Each time I close my eyes again, I'm immersed back into the nightmare to relive all over again.

CHAPTER FIFTEEN

Together

Three Weeks Later

Luke has been very persistent in trying to get me naked and beneath him. It's been the worst struggle not to succumb to his advances. I keep telling him that he needs to heal, and when we finally are together, I don't want to have to be careful and watch how I move or what I do. Not that I'm rough in bed or anything, but I know if I see him wince I won't be able to keep going. Plus, I wouldn't mind it if he was a little rough with me.

The first week after the confrontation with King Pine, we remained inside Luke's home, much to his dismay. He wanted to be out there doing things, although what, I don't know. There was nothing important he had to tend to. Elliott came by often to check on him, and I grilled him about what was going on, so I could put Luke's mind at ease that he wasn't needed at the moment. However, it only seemed to piss him off that his men didn't need him. I'm quickly learning that he always has to be doing something. Being sedentary doesn't work for him, injured or not.

Week two we went outside in the courtyard a lot. We had a few meals with his brothers and sister. We did some shopping and visited with different people who live in the kingdom, mostly Elite members and their wives.

The third week we got adventurous since Luke was feeling better. We took out his horse and he showed me around the land. We had a picnic near the old cottage where I entered this realm. I could see the look of longing in his eyes. He wanted to see his mother again. We aren't sure if they'll return. For all we know, the key could have disappeared when he went through. Or he couldn't get ahold of his wife. There are so many things that could go wrong. I wish there was a way we could find out, but the only thing that happens when I open the door to the cottage is me ending up in a dirty, old space. Only with the key in the lock and turned can you open the portal back to my apartment.

Right now, I'm lying in bed in nothing but a pair of panties. I showered and threw on one of Luke's shirts, the only thing I'll wear to bed. As soon as I heard the water in the shower come on, I stripped out of it. I left the damask open on the side of the bed facing the bathroom. I'm lying on my side, waiting for him to emerge. I only hope he finds me irresistible when he does. He's been all but begging me to let him touch me outside of some heated make out sessions. It hasn't been easy, but I think the wait will definitely have been worth it. He has no idea he'll find me like this when he opens the door. I want to surprise him.

While I wait for him, my mind wanders back onto all of the sweet moments we've had. He does always find ways to touch me or hold me close. He will kiss me no matter where we are or who's watching. I love how attentive he is, and how much he wants everyone to know I'm his. Not that I think any of the local men would be fighting him to have me. There are some people who still look at me as a traitor, even though I've never given them reason to believe so. I guess being the daughter of King Pine is enough for them. The only competition Luke would have is Oliver, and we haven't seen him since he left the night of my father's death.

Two nights ago he took me to where the dragons sleep at night and walked me to Tali's stall. I thought he was going to take me for a ride on her, but boy was I surprised. Tali came walking out and nudged me with her big, horned head, careful not to hurt me. Then right behind her appeared a smaller dragon, whose color reminded me of a storm cloud on a hot summer day. It seems Tali was busy. She and Elliott's dragon were found sound asleep inside her area one morning. Luke had said she was a loner, but I guess she got sick of it, and there we were with a baby dragon. Who knew how long the other dragon had been visiting her for? Elliott and Luke both decided he would become mine. My own dragon. What the hell I need a dragon for is beyond me. They both insisted, though. Even Addison had one.

I couldn't help but fall in love with the little guy. Little being the wrong word, really. He was bigger than a full-size SUV. He came right up to me and ran around me in circles. I named him Storm after the first thing I thought of when I saw him. The name seems to fit. He's been a terror with the other dragons. Teasing them and trying to get them to play with him. Fortunately, they all put up with him really well. Of course, I think it helps that Tali would harm any of them that hurt her son. She is the most powerful dragon of any they have and none test her.

There are days I still can't believe I'm here and living this life of fantasy. Luke alone is a man that only my dreams could conjure up, yet he's very real. Add in seers, that dragons really exist, and all kinds of other things I have yet to see for myself.

Luke tells me stories of other creatures beyond the woods and the other kingdoms that exist in this realm. He says one day we can travel and see everything. It seems the only kingdom the Azures had warred with is Pine. The other kings all have a peace treaty and no battles are fought between them, nor would they back either Azure or Pine in war. They designed the treaty to avoid bringing conflict to other borders. We still don't know what's going on with the Pine leadership. Luke assumes Reid has taken over.

The doorknob turning with a click draws my attention back to the bathroom and the man I'm waiting for. He steps out shirtless in all of his chiseled glory. The muscles on his stomach form little mountains that I can't wait to explore with my tongue. They lead down to the V at his waist, like an arrow pointing where I should go, and oh, will I ever. His hair is damp and sticking up haphazardly. Navy, cotton shorts hang low on his hips. There is jagged scar running across his chest that makes my heart hurt every time I lay eyes on it.

One step into the room and he freezes. His eyes widen and his mouth forms an O. He takes a moment to let his gaze rake over my body. His eyes burn a path from my toes to my chest with each inch he takes in. When he gets to my bare breasts, he stops. His tongue snakes out to lick his bottom lip. My legs squeeze together to try and ease the ache that's forming.

His eyes meet mine and they smolder with intensity. He walks to me like a jungle cat on the prowl. As he approaches the bed, I start to move over giving him room. With speed I don't know he has, he's by the bed and climbing on top of me before I can move. His arms brace on either side of my head, locked tight to keep his weight off of me. He's kneeling, straddling my legs. My breath is coming out in pants at the anticipation of what's to come.

Before he touches me, he asks, "Are you sure? Once you give yourself to me there's no going back."

"We've already crossed that point the night you were hurt. I don't want to go back, only forward. And only with you."

He leans down to feather a kiss over my cheek. "My princess," he whispers in my ear. Goosebumps break out over my skin when he begins to kiss a trail from the spot just below my ear, down my neck to my shoulder. He doesn't stop there, only continues a path until he reaches my breast. His tongue flicks over the sensitive peak, drawing a moan from deep within my throat. How I've wanted his mouth on me; how I've craved this very moment.

He takes my nipple between his teeth and gently bites down. My back arches off the bed as pain and pleasure mix, fueling the fire building inside me. His hand finds my other breast and kneads it with his strong fingers. I want more of him. I want all of him.

Releasing my breast, his lips journey south past my navel to the juncture of my thighs. He hooks his fingers inside my panties, drawing them off so slowly it's torturous. Gentle hands skim up the inside of my legs, only to stop short of where I want them most.

"So beautiful," he murmurs. "All mine."

Leaning down, his tongue sweeps between my folds, drawing a cry from my lips. Zaps of electricity race through me from that single touch.

"So sweet," he speaks against me.

He presses firmly against my clit and alternates between sucking and licking. I try to squeeze my legs shut and lift my pelvis from the bed. The sensation is too much, and not enough at the same time, but he's relentless in his pursuit to drive me to ecstasy. His hard as steel body is between my thighs, and one arm is over my stomach to hold me down. His pace quickens. He moans against me. I begin to writhe beneath him, my orgasm imminent. When he inserts two fingers inside of me, I crash over the edge, helpless to hang on any longer.

My body spasms as my orgasm tears through me. Luke doesn't stop. He wants to pull every bit from me that he can. I'm calling out his name over and over. I've never experienced anything like this. I'm hot all over, sweat beading on my brow. As soon as I start to come down, he picks up the pace, pushing me toward the brink again. I can't take much more. I want him inside of me. Need him there like I need air to breathe.

My fingers grip his hair to pull him from me. He stops after my fourth attempt at doing so. I'm left weak, but ready for more.

He's over me again, lowering himself to me. I feel the head of his cock at my entrance, and I lift my hips to bring us closer faster. As he's about to push in he stops. "Ali, have you been drinking the tea

Stephanie left for you?" Seriously? He wants to talk to me about tea right now?

"Ummm...I have, but I don't quite understand why you're asking me about that at this very moment."

He chuckles. "She didn't tell you what it was, did she?" I shake my head. "It's a tea to prevent you from becoming pregnant."

"What? They make a tea that does that? Get the hell out." Who would have thought? I wonder why it's not used back home. "Wait. Why didn't she tell me what it was for? She said to drink it daily to keep me healthy and to talk to her before stopping it."

"I don't know. She probably knows something we don't. That concerns me a little."

"Let's have this talk another time. Right now, you're here. I'm here. And I want you badly."

Reaching down, I grasp his length in my hand, causing him to suck in a breath. I watch him close his eyes as I slowly stroke him. He's hard in my hand and I need him to be inside of me. Lifting my hips again, I bring him to my center. His eyes flutter open when he touches me. He gazes down and we lock eyes as he enters me.

My body tenses at first, then stretches to accommodate him. He's large, and I haven't been with anyone in quite some time. Once he's fully settled into me, he sags against me and shudders.

"You feel so good. So right. So perfect," he rasps.

He kisses me, and the second our tongues touch, I wrap my legs around him. Slowly he moves, but I want it faster, harder.

"More," I plead against his lips.

He picks up the pace, then brings his arms around me to pull me into a sitting position with him. His legs are beneath me and we're face-to-face. I love this connection I have with him. I've never known anything like it. It was something I felt since I've first met him, but now it's like everything has aligned, and we're where we're meant to be. The whole fate thing he speaks of is resonating now.

Tucking a hair behind my ear, he speaks softly, "My princess. My heart."

I kiss him deeply and hope it conveys the depth of what I'm feeling. He holds me tight to him. I start to move up and down. We break the kiss. My head falls back and he kisses along my neck. His hands grip my hips, his fingers biting into my skin, moving me the way he wants. I'm happy to relinquish control. I want nothing more than for him to possess every part of me.

Leaning back further, I brace my arms behind me and Luke finds my nipple, sucking it into his mouth. His thrusts, his tongue, my orgasm is quickly building. I lay all the way back, while my hips still rest in his lap. He rises to kneel on the bed, holding my lower body in the air. With a strong grasp of me, he quickens his pace and powers into me. I'm dizzy with sensation.

His thumb finds my clit and starts rubbing in small circles. Within minutes I'm crying out his name, convulsing in his hands. He rides me through and doesn't join me until I start to come down from my high. With a few strong thrusts, he tenses, then covers me with his body to release himself inside of me.

We roll to our sides. I lightly drag my nails through his hair, while my lips rain kisses over his face. I want to live in this moment forever. It's only us, connected, together, as intimate as two people can be, and it's amazing. Earth shattering. Euphoric.

"Was I worth the wait?" I ask, teasing him.

"I would wait my entire life to be with you if I had to. Every day I have you in my arms is a treasure. One I don't take for granted. You're meant for me, Alison. You're my soul mate. Our connection flares to life when we're together. Please tell me you felt it, too."

Quietly, I admit, "I did. I do."

We spend the rest of the night wrapped in each other. There are short moments of sleep in between, but I am woken up by his lips or his hands. When the night turns to day we keep the damask closed and come together over and over. Finally emerging from our little nest, my body is deliciously sore, and I'm floating on a cloud.

CHAPTER SIXTEEN

Treaty

About a week later, at least I think it was a week later. Honestly, I have no concept of time anymore. I know when to wake and I sleep when I'm tired. I eat when I'm hungry. Luke laughs at me since I'm still trying to get used to functioning this way.

Anyway, about a week later Elliott knocks on our door with news. Yes, our door, because I never did look for another place to live. Luke wouldn't even listen any time I brought it up, and I'm very content to sleep next to him every night. So I gave in and very happily at that.

He answers the door, and we find Elliott on the other side with a tense jaw and a frown. "What's going on, brother?" Luke asks.

"We've been invited to dinner with King Pine." I

suck in a breath. I know my father is dead, but hearing that name rocks me for a second. "Reid Pine," he clarifies. "Apparently, he wants to discuss the peace treaty and spend some time with his sister."

Luke's body has gone rigid beside me. I see his face mimics his brother's. "Does Ry know?"

"Yes, I just came from seeing him. He's going, but is leaving whether or not you both want to attend up to you."

"I have to go. Ali, you don't."

"I don't understand why you both are so tense," I say. "My father is dead. When everything went down I remember him saying that Reid wasn't like him. That he likes to avoid conflict. I wouldn't mind getting to know him." I drop my eyes to the floor and speak softly. "He's the only family I have left. I want to go."

Luke steps closer and gathers me in his arms. I take comfort in his strength. "He's not your only family. You have me and Elliott. All of the Azures are your family now." Tears prick the back of my eyes, but I blink them away. "If you'd like to go, then we'll go. Brother, please respond that we'll attend, but will be bringing the Elite with us. Also, I want his word, and that of Sage, that no harm will come to any of us. We're going for a meal and to hopefully get this treaty signed. If I feel Ali is in danger, I will not hesitate to protect her."

Elliott replies through clenched teeth. "I'm not happy about going into their land, but as you wish."

Luke's chest deflates against me. "If what Reid says is true, then we have to be willing to discuss it. We've wanted peace with them for so long. Maybe now that Rafe is gone we'll be able to attain it."

"I don't think he, and especially not Sage, would harm Ali, but I don't trust them. Any of them."

"Neither do I," Luke states.

Four days later we're on the back of Tali flying to the Pine Kingdom. The Elite surrounds Ryland on his dragon, and Luke and me on his, with Elliott at the front. Storm is much too small to carry anyone, although he is growing quickly, and wasn't happy to be left behind. Addison said she would keep him occupied. He loves to play. I'm sure he's loving the extra attention.

My nerves have been doing a number on me all day. I've barely been able to eat, which isn't normal for me, and my hands shook as I tried to tame this wild mane of hair I have. Luckily, Addison was there to braid it for me. She's very skilled. I've never been able to make my hair look like it does. The braid goes from the base of my hairline on the back of my neck, upward and ends in a bun on top. She made me look elegant. It will also serve to keep my hair from becoming a knotted mess from the flight.

I decided to wear a pair of tight, azure colored pants tonight, with a loose white blouse. I would have loved a skirt, but that's not really easy to wear while traveling by dragon. I also had a local leather craftsman make me a pair of tall, low-heeled boots. They are black and lace all the way up, hugging my legs perfectly. I put them on to complete my outfit. We may be going to a dinner with a king, but I myself am a princess and will dress how I see fit. Plus, Luke said that very rarely does anyone dress in big ball gowns or overly formal attire. He told me I read too many books in my previous life.

My previous life. The more I'm here, the more I feel like I wasn't really living when I was back in the States. This place, this realm, it's nothing short of magical. The creatures I'm discovering, the dragons, the people, and most of all – my prince.

Tali banks to the right along with the rest of the clan, and we start our descent. There are tall pine trees below us. They become denser the closer we get to the castle. The castle looks much like the Azure one, but this one isn't surrounded by water, only a dense forest of pine trees. There is a large flag atop their tower house, which is evergreen in color; the head of a black wolf appears on it as it billows in the breeze.

We touch down just outside of the main entrance. Tali rears up as men approach us. Luke shouts for them to stay back. Elliott is off his dragon, running up to stand before us, and pushes the men back. I've learned that Tali is very intuitive. She senses danger, tension, and other emotions. Luke explained it's one of the reasons she's the leader of their clan. He's hoping Storm inherits her traits. All the better to protect me, he says.

With the men far away from Tali, she calms, and we're able to jump down. I've become more agile and fit since being here. I no longer need Luke's help to get on Tali's back or get down. My body was always lean, but I'm packing on muscle. We go for runs together. He's even been sparring with me. I have to admit, it's a lot of fun.

One of the Elite hangs back to stay with the dragons, while Ryland, Luke, Elliott, seven Elite, and myself walk through the main doors leading to the courtyard. Pine guards surround us, escorting us forward. One step in and Oliver is waiting for us. His dirty blond hair is styled back from his face. He's wearing black twill pants that fit him in the waist, and a deep green, long-sleeved fitted shirt. He's cleanly shaven and reminds me of a guy I'd find back home. Those hypnotizing green eyes hone in on me and a gentle smile graces his face. He takes a few steps forward, meeting us halfway. He doesn't give more than a passing glance to Ryland. I smile in return and reach out to embrace him. His arms wrap around me as he holds me carefully. Not wanting anyone to get the wrong idea, I pull back and clasp Oliver's hands in mine.

"It's nice to see you again, Oliver."

"You're more beautiful than I remember, Princess. I'm very happy to have you here with us. Come, let's go find your brother."

He offers his arm and I don't know if I should take it or not. Luke and I discussed seeing Oliver again. He knows how much Oliver wants me as his, but my choice is made and won't change. I look back to my prince, who inclines his head, silently telling me it's all right to take his arm. While I don't need his approval to do anything, I would want him to extend the same courtesy if it were the other way around. I turn back and see Oliver and Luke have locked eyes. I loop my arm through Oliver's and tug him forward. I don't want these two fighting, especially over me.

We all walk inside the walls; immediately I notice it isn't as bright and lively as Azure is. There are only a handful of vendors and they watch us with open curiosity. I would have thought they hated us, but maybe my father wasn't a great leader. He could have treated his people like shit, for all I know, and they are happy Luke killed him. Also, we don't know what Reid has said about us to them.

Arm-in-arm, Oliver and I lead the men through the courtyard. I take a quick look at Ryland. He seems content to follow for the time being. He dressed in a deep navy, long-sleeved shirt paired with black twill pants. We get to the tower house where we walk past guards and finally into a grand dining room. There is a long wooden table with a feast spread out. The walls are decorated in shades of green and their crest is prominent on the wall.

The only man in the room is Reid, my male mirror image. His dark hair is tousled in a way I'm sure he intended. He first extends his hand to Ryland and they exchange pleasantries. I don't believe they've met before this. From what Luke has said, Ryland steers clear of the battlefield. He said he's not meant to fight, only rule. Yet, King Azure does both and so did the previous King Pine. Even Reid dressed in armor that day at the border.

Next, Reid turns to me. He smiles, takes a step forward, but stops. Luke and the rest of his men stop behind me. He's so close to my back I can feel heat coming off of him. Oliver scowls next to me and I swear Luke growls. Seriously, these are grown men behaving like animals. I'm not anyone's property!

I step out of Oliver's grasp, away from Luke's warmth, and forward to my brother. He's wearing an outfit almost identical to Oliver's, but Reid's shirt is a lighter green. I'm unsure of how to greet him. We didn't have any time to talk or get to know each other. Leaning in, I give him the most awkward hug of my life. I can only imagine what the two of us look like. Maybe two guys trying to hug it out, certainly not family. I pat him on the back and pull away. Glad that's over.

"Alison, I'm so happy you've come," Reid says smiling. Luke steps up beside me, Oliver on the other side. I resist every urge I have to roll my eyes. "Prince

Lucas," Reid addresses Luke. "Thank you for coming. And you as well, Prince Elliott. Let's sit and eat before the food gets cold."

We all take seats at the table. Being Reid's sister, I'm offered the seat to his left and Ryland takes the one opposite me. Elliott sits beside Ry, then Oliver next to him, and Luke takes the chair on my other side. The rest of the Elite sit down wherever they want. There are four Pine guards within the room as well. They stand along the walls quietly.

We begin our meal and conversation is kept light. About the time dessert is served, we turn the talk to the peace treaty.

"As you know," Reid begins. "My father never wanted to sign the treaty. I tried on many occasions to persuade him, but it couldn't be done. After my mother, our mother," his eyes find mine for a moment and his face becomes somber, "left, my father changed. One of our seers came by and told him how our mother had a baby girl and had no plans to return, even though she held the key. As you can imagine, this didn't go over well with him. His mood shifted and he became ruthless. He lashed out at anyone who disagreed with him. He treated our people terribly. Food wasn't abundant for those in lower standing. He killed a man right in front of everyone for stealing a loaf of bread to feed his family." I draw in a sharp breath as he continues, noting my expression. "I won't go into more detail. But he was on a tirade for a long time." I'm glad I didn't have to live through that and was with my mother. I wonder if him not signing the treaty was one of the reasons my mom left. She and I were a lot alike, as is Reid. All peacekeepers.

"With your father gone, you feel like the time is right to sign?" Ry inquires.

Reid nods while swallowing the bite of food he has in his mouth. "I think it's what our people want and know it's what I want. Alison and I are the only members of our family left. I have to do everything in my power to keep the peace between our two kingdoms. I don't want any more war. No more death. I want us to all coexist, like you do with the other kings. Once we're through here I'll be approaching the other kings to ensure peace all around, but it starts with Azure." Luke had explained to me that Azure wasn't the only kingdom Pine went to war with. His was just hit more often than the others.

"I'm happy to enter into an agreement with you," Ry states.

Reid smiles. "Good. Let's have dessert, and then we can go through the agreement and sign."

A couple of women with emerald colored dresses enter the room with dessert trays. The Elite start chatting it up with Oliver and learning about each other's army.

I take this chance to ask Reid the question I've been wondering the answer to. "Reid, how old are you?" Luke reaches beneath the table to give my leg a squeeze. We've both been quiet up until this point.

Reid smiles. "I'm twenty-eight."

"Four years older than me." He nods. "Do you remember Mom?" The question is blurted out with no thought whatsoever. Shit. I watch his face drop a little. This can't be an easy topic for him.

"Barely. I have a few memories and they are mostly good. Her singing to me, putting me on her back and hiking. I also remember her leaving and crying myself to sleep for many nights. Dad was of no comfort, and I was pretty much left with a nanny to soothe me. I retreated into myself a lot and blamed him for her leaving. If he didn't need to war with everyone, maybe she would have stayed." I reach over and grasp his hand in mine to give him a gentle squeeze.

"I think there was more than one reason she left," I say, stopping there. No way was I going to divulge about King Azure and Rya.

"She's...she's gone, right?"

"Yes. She died about a year ago. I only found the key the day before I came here."

He gives me a small smile. "I know. The seer told me. Once Father knew you were alive, he stopped asking about Mother. I didn't, though. Once a year, on my birthday, I went to see Anna, our seer, and asked her about you and Mother. She had said something about her passing, but I stopped there. I didn't want to hear anymore. I instead switched to you. I knew she was going to die and that you would come. I just had to bide my time. I didn't tell father. Anna did. I didn't even know he still sought out information about you."

"I'm sorry you didn't get to know her. I have a picture of her back at Luke's. Next time we meet, I'll bring it so you can see. We both look so much like her."

"You want to see me again?" he asks with surprise in his voice.

"Yes," I smile. "Of course. You're my brother. I missed out on knowing you all my life. We have a lot of time to make up for."

He gives me a wide smile. "I'd like that."

After dessert Ryland and Reid go into a separate room. I take this opportunity to pull Oliver aside and ask him a question I didn't want to ask in front of everyone.

"Why didn't you leave? Why did you stay with such an awful man as your ruler?"

"It's not that simple. I couldn't leave. For one, where would I go? Any outside kings would see me as a spy. They wouldn't trust me enough to let me within their walls. And if Rafe found out I left, he'd have his men hunt me down and would kill me himself for betraying him. As you know first-hand, he didn't take well to those who went against him. But above all of that, I stayed, because I was waiting for you." My eyes close as emotion builds in my chest. He continues, "Princess, above everything else, I want you to be happy. Even if that means you're with Lucas." His lip curls slightly when he speaks Luke's name. I don't get a chance to respond, however, because Reid and Ry return with a signed treaty in hand. That was quick.

I hug my brother and promise to see him again soon. He shakes hands with all of the Elite, as well as the Azures. Oliver escorts us back through the front entrance of the castle's surrounding wall. He shakes hands with everyone including Luke, who then takes a few steps back to give us some space. He knows he has nothing to worry about, but I think he's still a little unsure where Oliver is concerned. He knows he won't hurt me, but I think he's afraid I'll be taken from him

"I'm sorry we didn't get to talk longer tonight," I say sincerely to Oliver.

"It's okay. I got to see you and that's what matters. Although, I'm not happy to see you go. Are you sure you won't reconsider my offer and join me here? You have no idea how elated you would make me, Princess. Reid as well." He knows how to pull at my heartstrings, however my place isn't beside him.

"I belong with Luke, Oliver." He closes his eyes briefly and lets out a breath. I guess it was too much to hope he had let go of this want to have me, even after our short conversation about him wanting me to be happy. Maybe one day he'll let go.

He brings me in for a hug. His lips brush my ear as he whispers, "Farewell, my beautiful princess. I'll keep hoping that one day you'll come to me."

"Oliver, please don't," I reply quietly.

He pulls back and I have to turn away. I don't feel awkward; I'm hurting him and I hate it. I don't want him to see the pain on my face. So I place a quick kiss on his cheek and turn to leave.

Together, Luke and I walk to Tali. She lies on the ground, ready for us to climb on. Once we're settled on her back, Luke wraps an arm around my waist, drawing me as close as possible and kisses me on the cheek. "Let's go home."

I lean my head back on his shoulder. "I'd like that."

We take to the skies and I look down upon the tall pine trees that surround the castle. I watch as Oliver stands, unmoving, with his head tipped toward us until we soar out of sight.

CHAPTER SEVENTEEN

Surprise

We land on the cliff at the edge of the Azure castle wall. All of the riders ensure their dragon's comfort before leaving, including us. I look into Tali's area and see Storm curled up in the corner with Addison asleep by him. Tali snorts, waking Addi. She jumps, but fortunately doesn't disturb him. Tali gives her a nudge as she walks past. The three of us walk out together.

"Thanks for staying with him tonight," I say.

She waves her hand absently in the air. "It was nothing."

We've kind of grown on each other. I wouldn't say we're besties or anything, but there is a mutual respect and a friendship. I think she does it for Luke. It makes him happy to see us get along, and whatever makes him happy, makes us happy. Hopefully, we can continue growing our relationship.

Luke gives her a playful shove as we stop to go inside his home. She waves and catches up with Elliott, who's only a few steps ahead of us.

Once inside, I let the comfort of our home wash over me. This is my safe space. It's where Luke and I can truly be alone. It's not a big space, but it's ours and I love it. Luke reaches around my back, drawing me to him. His lips crush down on mine as he takes possession of my mouth. I go weak in his arms. My own wrap around his neck to help hold me up before my legs give out. He has that kind of effect on me.

He pulls away, but only a fraction. "I've wanted to do that all night," he admits.

"Take me to bed."

His lips lift in a smile. "Your wish is my command." He bends down, lifting me into his arms with ease. I rest my cheek against his shoulder as my arms hold on. He takes the stairs quickly. Upstairs, he delicately places me on the bed and pulls the damask closed around us.

"It's only us now. Just the way I like it," he says, while placing kisses along my neck. Reaching down, I grip the hem of his shirt and lift it over his head. I make quick work of his pants and briefs as well. My hand grips his length hard, eliciting a moan from him. He's heavy, solid, and perfect.

Pushing on his chest, he rolls to his back,

bringing me on top of him. I strip off my shirt and bra, throwing them to the side. I'm craving my connection with him. Slow won't work for me right now. I need him badly. Kneeling above him, I start to pull off my pants and silk underwear, which I had especially made along with my bra. The basics the vendor offers just don't cut it for me.

Straddling him, I grip his length and slowly lower myself to him. My head tips back and I let out a moan of satisfaction. It's as if I'm not whole until we're connected to one another. Then, and only then, do I feel like everything is perfect in the world. Luke is all I need to survive. He's imperative to my well-being, but not because of his protection of me. No, he's everything I need wrapped up into one person. One man who is mine and mine alone. The air is crisper when he's around. The sky is bluer and the grass greener. He's my dream come true. Literally. There's no limitation to what I can do with him by my side. I feel like a new woman, a better woman.

His hands grip my hips, and quickly roll me over, as we jockey for position. I'm thankful for his king-sized bed or else we'd be on the floor. He begins to thrust into me in deep, languid movements.

"You. Are. Mine," he says between each pump of his hips. "Mine, Ali. Do you hear me?"

He bends to take my nipple into his mouth, biting down just the way I like. My back arches off the bed as electricity shoots from my breast straight to my core.

"Say it, Alison. Say you're mine." He's flicking my nipple with his tongue in between bites, and it's driving me wild. My heels dig into his firm ass, pulling him to me.

Breathily, I rasp, "I'm yours, Luke. Always."

He brings his mouth to mine and plunges his tongue within. He's pumping into me faster. My nails are scoring his back. His fingers fist my hair, pulling it, giving a quick, sharp pain as he tries to get deeper; his mouth more possessive. We're holding each other as if our lives depend on it.

I'm close, so close, but not able to get the sweet release I seek so desperately. Moving my hand down between us, I rub my clit, chasing after my orgasm.

We break our lips apart to gasp for air. "I love it when you touch yourself."

He lifts his head to look between us. I do the same and the sight is very erotic. His dick pushing into me, my hand furiously rubbing over my swollen nub. It sends me soaring. My eyes close as my body spasms in the most blissful way.

Luke is powering into me and two hard thrusts later he calls out my name. His body tenses as he fills me. He draws out his orgasm, and mine, with a few more pumps of his pelvis before relaxing on top of me, yet keeping the majority of his weight from me.

His skin is slick against mine. We're both out of

breath and our hearts are racing. He rolls us to our sides, then reaches over to open the damask to let the semi-cool night air in. I've noticed that while the days are warm, so are the nights, but my body is getting used to it. Where I was warm all the time when I first arrived, now I'm wearing long sleeved shirts at night, and sometimes during the day, like everyone else.

He kisses along my jaw. I flex my inner walls to grip his softening length. "I love it when you do that," he murmurs.

"I love it when you're inside of me." And I love not having to use a condom with him. It makes everything all the better. We feel everything. I admitted to not being with anyone in quite a while, and he confessed the same. He said once he started dreaming of me, no other woman could compare. I've seen the way women flirt with him. It happened a lot when I first arrived, but he quickly tempered it down by telling them he wasn't interested and showing affection to me when we were out.

We did find out from Stephanie that she asked me to drink the tea, because she knew we would be sleeping together soon. This way we wouldn't have to worry about me getting pregnant. She also said I'm very fertile and to keep drinking the tea until we're ready for kids. Kids. I'm so not there yet.

The moonlight is falling upon the bed. I can see the hard planes of Luke's body and the strong angles of his face as he pulls back to look at me. He cups my cheek with one hand, gently rubbing his thumb over my skin.

Our eyes lock and he speaks so quietly I almost don't hear him. "I love you, Alison."

Tears form in my eyes. He loves me. This gorgeous prince loves me. Boring Alison from middle of nowhere Colorado. Emotion clogs my throat and I bury my face in his neck. I can't speak. Not yet at least. It's too much, more than I thought it would be if I ever heard him utter those words. He holds me tight, his hand loosening the bun from the back of my head, running his fingers through my hair until it's lying at my back.

Never would I have thought I could fall for someone so quickly, but I have. He deserves to hear those words from me as well. Not because he said them and I feel obligated to reciprocate, but because I mean them.

"I love you, too," I murmur into his skin, as I kiss a path from his collarbone to his chin. "I love you so much it scares me."

He pulls back to look me in the eyes. "I will never hurt you, Alison. You're the only woman I want. Please know this is the truth. You're all I need."

I nod as tears run hotly down my cheeks. He's become too important to me to ever let go. I'm glad the peace treaty was signed and there are no other kingdoms out there that could war with Azure. The thought of him going into battle makes my chest constrict.

"You have all of me, Luke. Heart, mind, body, and soul. I'm yours."

"And I'll protect you with my life," he says seriously.

We touch, kiss, and profess our love with our bodies, all through the night, until we both fall asleep in each other's arms while the sun starts to rise in the sky. Luke pulls the damask closed as I begin to fall into a peaceful sleep.

◆

The next morning Luke finds my backpack and fills it with fruits, cheese, bread, and other necessities for a picnic. We walk to the stables and mount his gorgeous black horse. With a slow trot, we make our way to the field of azure flowers that I love so much. Picnics have become regular for us. A nice break to get away from everyone and everything.

We stop closer to the edge of the woods by the old cottage. Luke hops off first and offers his hand to me to help me down. Once on the ground, I pat the horse's neck then bend to run my fingers over the silky petals of the flowers. There's something so magical about them. They draw me to them, making me want to lay down in their beauty and never leave.

Reaching into my bag, he withdraws a large ivory

blanket. With a quick flick of his wrists, the blanket is spread out. The horse wanders off to the edge of the field, near the cottage, to eat the tall grass that's grown there. Luke takes the backpack, removes the food, and places it out for us.

I sit and he situates himself behind me, with his legs on either side of mine. Leaning into him, I take a minute to close my eyes and soak up the warm sun that's beating down on my skin. The sky is cloudless and the air is refreshing as it moves through my lungs. It's not long before I feel something cool against my lips.

"Open," Luke commands teasingly.

My lips part to allow a large grape inside. The tartness of the skin bursts open when I bite into it, allowing the sweetness of the inside to release into my mouth. I hum around the grape at the freshness of it. I've noticed everything here is so rich and full of flavor. Luke said all of the fruit is grown locally. He explained it one day when we flew with Tali while the sun was out. I saw orchards and vineyards in the land off to the east of the castle. Other kingdoms specialize in different items, and they barter with one another for goods. For example, one raises livestock and Azure exchanges vast amounts of fruit for beef, pork, and poultry. And that's only one of the deals they have.

He continues to feed me grapes, apples, and cheese as I absently draw circles over his inner thigh. It's very peaceful out here. The only sound is the occasional swish of the horse's tail or nicker he makes. But then, there's a new noise. A soft click followed by a dull thump. Luke's body goes rigid behind me. I sit up straight, looking around with wide eyes, trying to figure out where the sound came from.

I scan the area and stop near the cottage. The horse's head is up, its ears twitching. He's staring at the cottage. Luke stands and begins to walk toward it. I do the same, but he holds up a hand to stop me, and places his forefinger to his lips to ensure I remain quiet. The cottage is abandoned. It's old and dingy inside. Why would anyone be in there? Unless...

Luke strides closer, resting a hand along his steed as he passes by. His moves are silent. Bending down, he pulls a dagger from the strap on his leg. I've learned that he never leaves the house without at least one blade one him.

There's another thump, louder than before. The door shakes and then bursts open. Two figures emerge with large boxes in their arms obscuring their faces. They both look back to the door for a second, trying to each juggle the boxes in their arms.

Luke inches closer, making no sound. The first figure is tall and stocky with hair that is oddly the same color as Luke's. No, it can't be. The box is placed on the grass and King Azure stands upright, tall and exuding power. His eyes immediately land on Luke and a huge smile spreads across his face. He rushes forward to grab his son in a tight hug. Luke's arms are by his side. I think he's in shock. I mean, we came here for a picnic. Never did we expect to see his dad. I start walking forward.

That's not all, though. There is another figure that came through. The box the person is holding is placed on the ground and Rya is revealed. Her dark blonde hair is shorter than I remember, cropped to just above her shoulders in a sophisticated bob. Her hazel eyes begin to pool with tears when she sees Luke. King Azure releases him.

His voice is full of disbelief. "Mom?" She nods and he rushes to her, lifting her in his arms. Rya is hanging on to him as sobs wrack her body. They stand holding each other for a moment then Luke takes a step back to look her over. "I can't believe you're here."

"Me either," she says, brushing tears from her face.

King Azure steps up to me and encompasses me in a bear hug. "Alison, my dear. I'm so happy to see you." He places me on the ground and the smile still hasn't left his face. "Have you been taking care of my boy?"

"Huh?"

He laughs heartily. "We surprised you, I take it."

"Little bit. You returned and brought Rya?"

"That I did. Oh, and we brought a box of items for you. It's not much, but we grabbed the things we thought you'd want since we weren't sure if we'd have the key still after we walked through."

"And?"

He shakes his head. "It's gone again."

"Again?"

"I'll explain, but not here. We need to get back to the castle and round up the family."

He turns and we both watch as Rya takes Luke's face in her hands. They're talking quietly, but after a few minutes turn toward us. I walk forward and hug Rya.

"It's so good to see you, Ali. Thank you for giving the key to Miles."

She steps back, but her hands remain on my shoulders. Reaching up she captures the tears I didn't realize I was shedding. Seeing her makes me miss my mom so much. As if knowing what I'm thinking, she says, "I miss her, too. Every day."

I close my eyes and take a deep breath. My back heats and I know it has to be from Luke. He's the only one who can warm my skin like the sun. His arms wrap around me to cross over my waist. His presence is just what I need to regain my composure.

"Come, my princess. Let's go spread the good news of my parents' return to my brothers and sister." I nod and open my eyes. Rya is watching us with a huge smile.

"A perfect match. I always hoped, but never knew for sure. You two are truly fated. Eliza and I wished one day you would find each other."

In a higher tone than usual, Luke asks, "You knew?"

She taps her temple. "I'm a seer, Lucas. Your father never told you?" I gasp.

"I had no idea. Did you know what happened after you left?" he questions.

She shakes her head solemnly. "No. Something happened when I left this realm. I lost my power. But I did have a vision before Eliza and I left. I saw you and Alison in this very field while horses ran past you, but as you know, there was no way to know if that future was the one that would come to pass." It was the day I crossed over. She saw it.

Luke released me and bent to pick up one of the boxes they brought through. "What's in this? Did you two plan how to get the boxes home?"

King Azure chuckles and clasps a hand on Luke's shoulder. "It was pure luck that you're here, my boy. You can carry one. I'll take the other. The women can ride on the horse."

"Or I can call for Tali," he says with a wicked gleam in his eyes.

"How?" I ask. "Do you have a whistle or something I don't know about?"

He laughs and taps his temple just as Rya did.

"My mom isn't the only one with talent. I only hope it works."

He closes his eyes, seeming to concentrate for a moment. Next we hear a muffled roar pierce the air. Within a couple of minutes, Tali is coming toward us with Storm following closely behind. The horse backs up a few steps as she lands gracefully before us. Storms lands as well, but hasn't quite mastered it yet. We all turn to look at Luke in surprise.

"What?" he shrugs. The king and Rya start walking away from us. "I don't know how it works, but it does. It started when Pine had the sword to your throat. All of the sudden, Tali was beside me, and we took to the air so I could drop in and surprise him. We're still working on communicating, but it's getting better."

"Why didn't you tell me?"

Another shrug. "It didn't come up."

I throw my hands in the air in defeat and step close to him. "No secrets between us. Got it?"

His wicked smile returns. "Yes, my princess."

He takes me in his arms and kisses me hard. When he releases me, I'm left dazed and half stumble toward the dragons. Damn, that man knows how to kiss.

CHAPTER EIGHTEEN

Reunion

King Azure and Rya are climbing on Tali's back with one of the boxes when Elliott shows up on his dragon. He lands with a ground shaking thump and jumps down. He runs toward Luke. "I heard Tali and took off after her. What's going on?" Luke inclines his head toward his mother. Elliott's jaw drop opens and he stands stunned.

"Dad? M...m...mom?"

Rya's hand reaches up to cover her mouth as tears fill her eyes again. She tries to speak, but her lip trembles too badly. Instead, King Azure addresses him. "Elliott," he says smiling. "Nice to see you."

Elliott runs to them as Rya gets down. She embraces her son. They both hold tight to one another for a few moments. King Azure places his hand on his son's shoulder. "Come, let's go home. Ali, grab a box and follow us. Luke, take the horse back. Elliott will watch over your girl."

Poor Elliott doesn't want to let go. Rya breaks apart first. I grasp his hand and gently pull him toward the black as midnight dragon. "The sooner we get back, the sooner we find out the details."

"Did you know they were coming back today?" he asks, shocked.

"No, we had no idea. Luke and I came out here for breakfast."

I look down once I'm on the dragon, and see Luke picking up our abandoned picnic and throwing the bag on his back. Elliott sits behind me with a box on his lap. I'm curious what was brought back for me and am wondering what will happen with my apartment and store. Although, does it really matter? I have no intention of ever going back even if I had the key, which I don't. We owned it outright, but with no next of kin or anything it will sit abandoned.

I watch Luke from above as we take off. He has the horse running at full speed. My prince on his brilliant horse. The sight of him makes my heart flutter. We'll beat him back to the castle, but hopefully not by much. People are going to be stunned when they see the king has returned with his queen in tow.

The flight back is quick. Tali lands first, with us

immediately after. Elliott's dragon doesn't have the same grace that Tali does, so we land a little rougher than I'm used to. Storm drops down behind us. I jump down, Elliott behind me with the box. We walk to stand beside King Azure and Rya. Elliott remains quiet as we go. The members of the Guard's eyes widen as we pass, but they say nothing. I wonder how many remember Rya. She's been gone for so long. We enter the walkway to the main courtyard. It's mid-morning, which means the castle will be bustling with vendors, workers, and others.

We enter the courtyard and walk briskly to the castle. Rya takes the box from the king and uses it to block her face. I'm sure they will address their people later on. First they need to reunite with the rest of their children and fill everyone in.

We enter the tower house and the guards immediately bow to the king. Inside the main dining room, Elliott quickly shuts the door behind us. He and Rya place the boxes on the empty table. He goes to her and they embrace.

"My son," she says. "I can't believe how big you've gotten." His face crumples with emotion. A lump forms in my throat as I watch his tears fall.

They talk quietly when the door opens and Luke comes through. Addison and Ryland enter behind him. They both stop in their tracks when they see their mother.

"Mom?" Addison cries. "Is that really you?" Rya

nods and Addi rushes to her, throwing her arms around her neck, and sobbing into her hair. Ryland approaches hesitantly. Rya holds out an arm and welcomes him into her embrace as well. Elliott is wiping tears from his eyes, along with King Azure. Luke steps up beside me and places his arm across my shoulders, pulling me close to him. We stand silent for a few minutes. The only sound in the room is Addi crying and the occasional sniffle from Elliott.

"Come, children," the king says in a soft voice. "Let's all sit and we'll tell you everything."

Everyone takes a seat. Addi refuses to let go of Rya's hand and I can't blame her. Had my mother come back I'd hold onto her with everything I have. Rya seems to barely be keeping it together. She takes the king's hand in her other one and nods, as he begins.

"When I went through the portal, I didn't know what to do or where to go. The key had disappeared. I wasn't sure if we'd get it back or not. I had Alison's instructions and found her phone to call your mother. She answered, then came to get me right away. I went with her to where she was living, since all of her belongings were there. We caught up and I learned a lot about the way things work on the other side. We hoped the key would return and it eventually did. But not until I got to see and experience some amazing things."

He turns to me and smiles. "You have such advanced technology where you're from. The cars and the televisions. Phones and computers. I was in awe of it all, but I knew if I did come back, none of it could come with me. I've seen what it's done to your world. How when people eat together they don't interact with one another. They drive with anger and are rushing everywhere they go. Our life may be simple here, but I like it that way."

"Me, too," I agree.

"What about the twins?" Luke cuts in. Rya's eyes close and her head drops.

Solemnly, the king says, "They didn't make it. Your mother was bleeding badly and there was nothing the doctors could do. She lost the babies." Addi's cries grow louder. My heart breaks for everyone. Rya left in an effort to save her babies, and in the end she lost them and everyone in her family. Twenty-four years she was without them.

Ryland speaks up. "Why didn't you come back? Didn't you want us anymore?"

With a shaky voice, Rya answers, "Of course I did. The key, it wouldn't stay with me. Eliza tried giving it to me, she tried opening the portal with me beside her, she even tried opening it alone, but it didn't work. Every time the key got near the lock it would disappear. We'd always find it back in my little pewter jewelry box."

"The box you brought with you from our home," King Azure interjects.

"Yes. The key liked it in there, even if it never let

me hold it. Eliza was the only one who could, yet it wouldn't work. It wasn't meant for either of us. It laid in wait for Ali. There was nothing we could do. We were both stuck on the other side."

"Could you foresee losing the babies?" Luke asks. "Then you could have stayed here with us; you wouldn't have had to leave." The other siblings stare at her with wide eyes. I guess no one knew she was a seer.

"No. I've never been able to see my own path. Since the babies were part of me, I couldn't see theirs either."

I'm chewing on my thumb now. "If you were so close to my mom, why didn't you two live near each other? I wouldn't want to be far from my best friend, if it were me."

"We did live close to one another, even together for a bit. But with the babies gone and the key refusing me, I was depressed. I moved away in hopes that if I put some space between the door and myself I could move on. I never thought I'd come back here."

"We need to address the people tomorrow," Ryland says. "We also have to tell them about the peace treaty."

The king quickly turns to face him. "The treaty? King Pine signed it?"

"Well, thanks to Luke, the king did, but not the one you think. Reid is now king."

The king spins to face Luke. I'm surprised his head doesn't swivel right off his neck. Luke's face becomes tense, his jaw clenches. "He deserved to die."

King Azure raises an eyebrow. "He has since Leo was killed, but what happened to cause you to do it now?"

"He threatened to kill Ali. He had his sword pressed to her neck and blood...blood was dripping from the blade." His hands are in fists so tight on the table that his knuckles are white. I reach for one hand, rubbing it in attempt to relax him.

"He didn't want me to stay with Luke," I add. "He wanted me home with him and Oliver, and if not, then he preferred me dead. Luke, along with Elliott and Oliver, saved my life." I turn to Luke. "I can never repay them."

He reaches up to brush his thumb along my cheek. "If anything had happened to you, I wouldn't have been able to go on. You're my reason for living."

"Oh, enough already," Addi pipes in. "We get it. You're in love. We don't need to see it all the time."

The king chuckles. "Stop, my daughter. It's nice that Luke isn't so murderous looking all of the time. Besides, if you ever find your one true love you'll be exactly the same."

She scoffs and crosses her arms. "I highly doubt that."

Rya rests a hand on her arm. "It's in your blood dear. When an Azure falls, they fall hard."

Addi rolls her eyes. "Can we change the subject please? All of this mushy stuff is getting on my nerves."

"Yes, dear, we can. I have a lot to catch up on and want to hear everything. We also need to agree on a story to tell our people about where I've been since they've all believed I was dead. What did you tell them about Ali's sudden appearance?"

"Nothing really," Ryland says. "We only warned them not to harm her or treat her with hatred. You should have seen the looks they were giving her once they knew she was King Pine's daughter. We wanted to be open, but the whole lot of them were rude. Luckily, she quickly won them over with her personality. Oh, and the fact that Luke killed her father. That helped as well."

"We can say you were on a humanitarian mission that took you far from our lands. While there you fell and hit your head. You had amnesia and didn't know who you were," the king states.

"Why didn't we go looking for her after a while?" Elliott asks.

"We did, but she had wandered off in her confusion and we couldn't find her."

"For twenty-four years?" he asks incredulously.

King Azure throws his hands up. "I didn't say it

was a good lie, but it will have to do. I won't take any questions. I'll say what I have to say and leave with my wife." Their eyes meet. The love he feels for her is apparent.

We sit around the table and talk for an hour before I excuse myself and get up to leave. I walk out the door, gently closing it behind me, but am stopped by Luke's hand on my wrist.

"Where are you going?"

"Home. I wanted to give everyone some time to catch up. You haven't seen your mother in so long. This is time for you to be with your family and reconnect. Go back. Enjoy it."

He reaches up to cup my cheek. "It still hasn't sunken in yet. You're my family. You and everyone in that room." His hand slides from my face to intertwine with my fingers. "Come. Let's go home together."

"But, your mom."

"It's fine, Ali. My brothers and sister will keep her busy. Besides, our picnic got interrupted. Let's go have lunch. We'll be sure to be back in time for my father's speech, and then we'll have dinner with them."

"Are you sure? I don't want you to leave for me."

He squeezes my hand and releases it. "It's more than fine. I'll be right back." Stepping back through the door, I hear them talking, but can't make out the words. I feel bad that he would leave them when he just got his mom back to come home with me.

When he returns, he's holding one of the boxes King Azure and Rya brought back with them. I don't know if I'll ever be able to call her queen. I've known her, vaguely as it was, on and off my whole life. She was always just Rya.

"You have a box to open."

"I wonder what's in it." It could be anything. King Azure said they packed some things for me. I don't know what will happen to the building, but at the same time, I don't care. My mom had to have known I would go through the door and the chances of returning would be minimal. Maybe that's why she was so insistent that I continue to run things after she passed. She knew eventually I'd find the key. Although how, I have no clue. It was tucked under a fake bottom of a drawer. Maybe that's the reason the dresser was priced so high. But then again, if the key does what it wants, it could have found me eventually. Who knows? I can't spend my time obsessing over that key and the what if's in life.

My reality is that I'm now living in the Azure Kingdom with a man by my side who loves me as much as I love him. A man who would and has risked his life for me. Who loves with his whole heart. Who I'm lucky enough to call mine. Lucas Azure is the center of my entire world, and I wouldn't have it any other way.

EPILOGUE

Lucas

Nervous is an emotion I'm unfamiliar with. That is until I arrived out in the field today on the back of Talethla, with my entire future ahead of me. You see, I knew Ali was special from the first time I saw her. I dreamt of her standing in the very field I'm in now. The azure flowers surrounded her. Her onyx hair blowing around wildly. She was a vision then, and even more so now that I've had the pleasure of getting to know her intimately. I knew the first day she appeared, she was mine. How? Call it intuition, or fate, or whatever you will, but I knew. Now I stand with my brothers by my side, waiting for her to give me her hand in marriage.

My mother had an arbor built and took some of the colorful ivy off of the cottage that holds the portal between our realms. She wove it through the lattice of the white arbor to bring even more color to our wedding. Teal, pink, purple, and blue ivy winds around it in a way, which makes it appear magical. Nowhere else in our land does ivy grow with those colors. Only on the cottage.

We have a small church within the castle's walls, but Ali said she wanted us to marry in the field. It's her favorite place, well, besides my bed. Or maybe that's my favorite place. Either way, I told her we could get married wherever she liked.

On the opposite side of the arbor stands Addi and my mother. Ali and Addi have become close over the last year, and since her own mother isn't here, she asked mine to stand with her. I still see the sorrow in her eyes when she thinks of her and knew this morning would be difficult without her here to help her get ready.

As luck would have it, one of the items my parents packed for her before they returned was an antique pearl comb. Ali said her mother wore it on her wedding day and wanted her to wear it when she got married. She cried when she saw it. There were also a few photo albums, jewelry, and other items my parents thought she would like to have in the box. It's too bad we weren't able to go back and bring all of her things here. The key hasn't been seen since when my father opened the door with my mother behind him. Fickle thing it is.

As I stand here waiting for her to arrive, I can't help but think back to when I proposed to her. We went out for a ride on my horse. We decided to explore the woods. It had been raining on and off for days, however we saw the sun was out and decided to chance it. While out, the clouds opened up and we took shelter beneath the canopy of leaves, but were still getting wet.

Taking advantage of the moment, I started kissing her. I'm helpless to resist those plump lips of hers. She wanted to play, though, and took off running through the woods. No match for me, I quickly caught her, but in doing so slipped, and we both ended up on the muddy forest floor. I hovered over her and loved watching the heat build in her eyes. Her nipples puckered beneath her shirt. It took everything in me not to take her right then and there.

Leaning down, I moved to capture her mouth with mine, although I never got there. She took a hand full of mud and smacked the side of my face with it, then started laughing hysterically. There was no way she was getting away with that. I returned the favor, but instead of her face I smeared it all over her breasts. I wanted to touch her so badly, it gave me an excuse to do so.

She quickly bucked me off and tried to get away, but I wasn't letting her. We ended up smearing mud all over one another, all the while laughing uncontrollably. It was the most fun I'd ever had.

By the time all was said and done, we were both covered from head to toe in mud. I had Ali beneath me again, and I knew it was the right moment to propose to her. I had no ring, no speech prepared, but I knew I wanted to spend the rest of my life with her.

I looked down and even covered in mud, she was the most beautiful woman I'd ever seen. "Marry me, Alison Wescot," I said with humor in my voice.

She was still laughing. "You're not serious."

"I'm very serious." I steeled my features so she knew I meant it. "I want you forever by my side. I want to spend every day for the rest of our lives with you in my arms. I want to wake to your gorgeous smile and luscious body. I want you to be my wife."

For a moment, I thought she was going to say no or tell me how ridiculous it was to ask someone to marry them while lying on the forest floor caked in dirt, but she didn't. She beamed with the most radiant smile. "Yes, Lucas Azure. Yes, I'll marry you."

I kissed her hard for a moment before standing and bringing her up with me. Gripping her waist, I lifted her in the air and spun her. Her legs wrapped around my waist, and I ended up backing her against a tree to kiss her once more. I pulled away before we went further. The mud was fun, but I had no desire to get it in more delicate places.

We found the horse and rode back to the castle a mess. The sun had come back out by then and was drying the mud nicely. The looks on the two guards' faces when we returned was that of worry. They thought we'd been attacked. I explained to them that I was indeed attacked, but it was by my dear fiancé, not someone who was out to do me harm. It took a moment for it to sink in that I referred to her as my bride to be. Once they caught on, they both cheered and helped us from the horse.

After saying their congratulations, they took the horse from me to return him to the stables while Ali and I walked through the courtyard back to our home. It was mid-day and with the sun back out, the vendors returned. They watched us pass with open curiosity. We stopped in the middle of everyone and I shouted, "She said yes! She's going to marry me!" I was elated and couldn't resist. I held her hand in mine as everyone around us clapped and cheered.

Now, here I am, waiting for her to make it official; to make her my wife. A few moments later, Storm touches down with my princess on his back. My father is with her and takes her hand once he's on the ground to help her down. I'm able to see her dress and it sends a rush of heat through me. My dick is very appreciative of her appearance; however, this is not the time nor place.

Our weddings are similar to the ones Ali described that took place in her realm. She said her father would have walked her down the aisle, but since hers was dead, she asked mine if he'd do the honor. He proudly accepted. Do I regret killing Rafe? No, not in the least. It was a long time coming. Him holding a sword to my love's throat was the final straw.

Her brother and Oliver are in attendance. Reid offered to walk her down the aisle, but she said she would rather my father do it. She's become close to him and he, in turn, treats her like one of his own children.

Reid and Oliver are the only ones from the Pine Kingdom that came. Well, and guards for their king. Ali went back and forth about inviting Oliver, but I said inviting him is a sign of trust and alliance. We are two kingdoms united by blood now, and I may have wanted him here so he can, once and for all, stop pining for my princess. Although, I don't know if even the wedding will keep him from desiring her.

All of the men in the wedding are dressed in formal wear. Black slacks, white shirt, black jacket. We also wear an azure sash over our chests, but beneath our jacket. My father has his crown on and a cape that matches the sash. On my and Elliott's jackets are the crest that marks us as Elite, the lion head.

Ali spent weeks going back and forth with the tailor working on her dress. She wanted to combine her more modern style with an element that represented her life with me. I wasn't allowed to see it before today. She said it was bad luck, but it was well worth the wait.

As she walks toward me with her arm looped through my father's, I slowly look her over. Her hair is twisted up on top of her head, and she's wearing the crown her brother gave her prior to the ceremony. He had it altered for her. It's small, simple, and subtle. Perfect. In the middle of the crown it comes to a high peak with smaller peaks down either side. Each peak has a diamond at the top. In the center of the crown is a large, teardrop-shaped emerald to represent the Pine side of her. Evenly spaced away from the center, below each smaller peak, are square sapphires to represent the Azure side she's marrying into. Teardrop shaped diamonds hang from her ears.

Her dress is a crisp white with silver vines of leaves across the bodice down to her waist. The silver embroidery continues at the bottom of the dress with more vines. At the top of her breasts is a wide, azure sash which wraps around her chest to her back and falls to a wide panel of azure with more silver embroidery all the way down. The tie in the back crisscrosses then narrows into small buttons down to the end of the train.

She's a vision with eyes only for me. The sun is high in the sky without a cloud in sight. It's beaming down, illuminating her in a stream of light. Ali truly is an angel walking amongst us. Ever since she stepped into my world, nothing has been the same. She's made everything better, including me.

Before her my life was ruled by violence, hatred, and the duty of protecting my land. Ali showed me love and compassion; that fighting isn't the only way to resolve things. She showed me kindness by helping my family out when she hardly knew us. My princess risked it all and none of us will ever forget it.

With every step her smile grows. When she and my father stop before me, I have to try my hardest not to allow everyone to see how badly my hand shakes when I take hers in it. We turn, stand before the priest, and listen as he speaks of love and marriage. Then it's our turn to say our vows. I'm asked to go first.

I take a deep breath, face my beloved, and clasp both of her hands in mine. "Alison, my princess. Our journey began when you entered my dreams. Even from afar, I knew there was something special about you. With every dream I woke to the hope that one day you'd appear before me. Then you did. I couldn't believe you were real. Every day since then has been nothing short of magical. I'm the luckiest man alive to get to spend the rest of my life with such an amazing woman. I promise to protect you with my life, to love you like no other, and to give you everything your heart desires. I love you, Ali. Always."

She lets go of my hand for a brief moment to brush tears from her face. Then I watch as her chest rises and falls with her own deep breath. "Lucas, my prince. My world was dull before I met you. The first day I saw you in this very field, it was as if I had seen in color for the first time. You're strong, where I'm weak. You're brave, where I'm afraid. You know what

I need without ever having to voice it. And you accepted me as part of your family long before you asked me to be your wife. I vow to spend my life cherishing you as you cherish me. You're my forever, Luke. I love you."

Tears begin to sting my own eyes and I blink quickly to keep them at bay. Not that I would mind if everyone sees me cry, but I don't want to release Ali's hands. I need her touch; to feel her warmth as a reminder that this is real.

We face the priest again and listen as he finishes the ceremony. At his words, I wrap an arm around my bride's waist and kiss her with everything I have. I pour all of my love and lust into the kiss. This is our first kiss as husband and wife. I dip her back and don't let up until I hear Elliott hooting and hollering beside me. We break apart and I smile like a fool. Ali's face has a blush creeping over it and it's adorable.

As we begin to walk down the aisle, I look to each person in attendance. My family, Ali's brother, my Elite, royals from other kingdoms. Everyone came to wish us well. To see different kings and queens sitting together is a sight to behold. The peace treaties are holding strong. I can only hope we maintain these alliances for many years to come.

Storm and Tali are waiting for us when we reach the end of our guests. I sweep Ali up into my arms, lifting her to Tali's back. I step up and settle myself behind her. Tali turns to us and I mentally ask her to take us home. She gracefully takes flight with Storm on our tail. Together we fly off toward the castle and our future.

About the Author

Michelle Dare is a romance author. Her stories range from sweet to sinful and from new adult to fantasy. There aren't enough hours in the day for her to write all of the story ideas in her head. When not writing or reading, she's a wife and mom living in eastern Pennsylvania. One day she hopes to be writing from a beach where she will never have to see snow or be cold again.

Newsletter Sign-Up: http://eepurl.com/bt14zX

Connect with Michelle online at the following sites.

Facebook:
https://www.facebook.com/authormichelledare

Facebook Fan Group:
https://www.facebook.com/groups/daresdivas/

Twitter: https://twitter.com/michelle_dare

Pinterest:
https://www.pinterest.com/michelle_dare/

Amazon:
https://www.amazon.com/author/michelledare

Website: http://michelledare.com/